THE JETTY

Kate Leonard

For Alex

PROLOGUE

Sorted. Her life was exactly where it should be. Two bright kids. A solid house in a good area, good schools. A clever, ambitious husband. Friends, coffee dates, choir practice and book clubs. Holidays in France. A wardrobe full of clothes from the Boden catalogue and an Audi on the drive. Life was good, life was on track. The suburban dream. That's what she'd thought. And then it had all started to crumble with a phone call. How could she not have seen how tenuous it all was? Everything she took for granted had been hanging from a single delicate thread, suspended, vulnerable. Poised to fall if she let her attention waver. A simple sentence of six words had sent the whole edifice crashing down.

In another lifetime she'd been a multi-tasker, able to juggle kids, work, friends and parents with a light touch, keeping the balls in the air, dexterous and assured. Now the balls lay scattered at her feet. She didn't even see them. The gentle monotony of daily life was over. From the moment she'd answered the phone, she'd found herself on a different track, narrow and steep, heading downwards at vertiginous speed. Her husband resented her. Maybe he'd even started to hate her. She saw the bewilderment and hurt in her kids' eyes. Her business was failing and her home was no longer secure. Had she done the right thing by running away here to find a safe haven? Maybe she should have stayed, braved it out, fought for what she had.

Instead she had escaped to this wind-battered island in

the far north of Scotland, removed from danger but with no control over events. What was happening back home? When would it be safe to go home? Could she rebuild her ruined life? Or did she even want that life anymore? Wasn't it just an illusion? Everything she'd once valued was so superficial. Meaningless. She was a different person now.

She followed the path blindly, head down, stumbling occasionally on the heather roots. She was only vaguely aware of the sea, bellowing and rumbling as it slammed into the caves below. At the top of the cliff she paused to catch her breath, held her hair back with one hand and at last looked around her. It was a magnificent sight. The sky was an ever-changing dance of blue, grey, indigo and silver as the wind chased the clouds across it. Waves broke against the rocks, sending sheets of white into the sky. At her feet the grasses whipped back and forth relentlessly. She stepped closer to the edge to look at the pure white foam frothing and bubbling at the foot of the cliff. It looked deceptively soft, just like cotton wool. Tempting. So tempting. One more step... She gasped as a sudden gust of wind punched into her anorak, pushing her further forward and making her throw out her arms for balance. God, that was close! Shocked and scared, she retreated back hurriedly.

She turned instead to the wooden bench that sat forlornly a few metres back from the exposed cliff edge and sat, elbows on her knees and chin in her hands, gazing out to sea. Watching the waves build and crash had a strangely calming effect and she began to feel more positive. Anger started to replace fear. How dare he! How fucking dare he! She was not going to let him win. Maybe it was time to face the danger. The sky was turning black and rain was starting to fall, first gently, then in fierce horizontal waves. She pulled her hood over her head and stood up, ready to make her way back down the hill to the log cabin. As she glanced down she was surprised to see a figure making its way up the cliff path. Another person as crazy as me, braving this changeable weather, she thought. As the figure approached she saw it was a man, walking with a deter-mined, heavy tread. He was wearing black waterproof trousers and a black anorak. Sensible, she thought. Probably a local. She couldn't see his face, only the top of his uncovered head, as he wove a careful path through the heather. Very short hair, like a buzz cut. His shoulders were broad and powerful. Some-thing about the set of his shoulders was familiar. And where had she seen someone with that same military haircut before? As he rounded the last bend, he looked up at her and smiled. She smiled back, conspiratorially, ready to make some remark about fools braving the weather. Then she froze. Her memory clunked in. Now she knew exactly where she'd seen him before. Standing beside a shiny black car, arms folded across his barrel chest and his face impassive. And again leaning against a bar, his muscly arms barely contained inside his discreet black suit jacket. This was no coincidence. If he was here there was only one reason. He was here to kill her. She looked around wildly, searching for an escape. The path didn't go any further, but ended here, at the highest point of the cliff. To her left, the mer-ciless sea, pounding the rocks hundreds of metres below. To her right impenetrable gorse, broken only by rocky outcrops and treacherous bogs. And below her, a killer who was climbing the last few metres to where she stood, a grim smile still fixed on his massive face.

1

'I don't like broccoli', Davie whined, looking down at his Superman plate with dismay. 'It tastes funny. And it looks like trees.'

'Trees are good,' Jenny said. 'Trees are strong and tall. If you eat your broccoli you'll be strong and tall like a tree.'

'Yeah, and if you don't eat it you'll always be a weakling. And you'll never get your yellow belt,' said Jake, holding up his own forkful of broccoli with a mean grin.

'Jake! Don't tease your brother. Concentrate on your own dinner, please,' said Jenny, exasperated. She didn't like this cruel streak that her eldest son seemed to be developing. Was it normal for a ten year old to start asserting his authority over his eight year old brother? What had happened to her sweetly complicit boys? Davie did ask for it sometimes though, she admitted to herself. He does whinge a lot. I hope he isn't getting bullied at school.

'Davie, just eat a bit of the broccoli, there's a love. Eat it before it gets too cold'.

She started to stack the pots in the dishwasher and paused to gaze out of the French doors. The back garden was littered with toys and the two bikes lay abandoned on the lawn. By the back hedge the boys had started to build a den, using one of her old dustsheets, streaked with paint. How great to have kids that actually still play outside, she thought, smugly.

They both do karate, they whiz about on their bikes, they make things and use their imagination. She gave herself a mental pat on the back, thinking with more than a hint of superiority of her neighbour Sue's kids, glued to their tablets all day long. At least I'm doing some things right. She caught sight of her own reflection in the glass and examined it dispassionately. I'm doing OK, she thought. My hair looks good with the new blonde highlights. No real wrinkles yet. Weight fine. Boobs starting to sag a little, but nothing a good new bra wouldn't fix. Yes, I could conceivably still be called a yummy-mummy.

'Right boys, all done?' she asked. 'Yoghurt or fruit for pudding?'

She scraped the remains into the bin and wiped down the kitchen surfaces. She loved her kitchen. The sleek black units contrasted well with the chrome appliances and white walls. The trio of pearly lights overhead cast a beautifully muted light onto the kitchen island. Grey Moroccan-style tiles separated the kitchen space from the eating space, which had the same wood-effect tiles that ran through the rest of the house. It was her favourite room. She turned again to the boys. 'What homework have you still got to do?'

'I've done mine. It was maths. It was really easy,' said Davie.

'We didn't have any today,' said Jake, looking rather shifty.

Jenny gave him a shrewd look, but decided to let that one go. Pick your battles; this one isn't worth the fight. 'OK. You can play on the PlayStation for an hour, if you both play nicely. But it's Davie's turn to choose the game, remember!' she warned Jake, sternly.

'Oh Mum! He only ever wants to play Lego all the time. That's a girl's game!'

'No it's not a girl's game,' wailed Davie, instantly rising to the bate, his face turning red with emotion.

'Jake, if you can't play nicely with your brother you won't be playing at all. Off you go now.'

Right, she thought. I've probably got a whole hour before they start kicking off. Paul won't get back till late, as usual. She frowned. He was working late more and more often these days, leaving her to cope alone with house and home. But what did she expect? He was starting his own business, it was bound to be time-consuming. I just wish he'd get back in time to play with the boys now and again, though. OK, what shall I do with my precious hour? I could do the accounts. I should really do the accounts. I could start making our supper, get ahead. No, she decided. Sod it. It's 'me time'. I'll do a bit more painting. She hurried upstairs and happily changed into her paint-stained jeans and one of Paul's old shirts. She went into the small fourth bedroom, the one she used as her studio, put the canvas on the easel and stood back, assessing it critically. There was something wrong with the eye, she thought. He looks a bit sly, a bit sneaky. It's probably the position of the white dot. Or the curve of the eyebrow. She looked again at the photo of the little Jack Russel. She read intelligence, curiosity and playfulness in the expression. She saw immediately what she had to change, and went to the bathroom to fill her jam jars with water. Then she arranged her acrylic tubes on the side table and chose a nice fine brush from her bamboo roll-up holder. She sighed contentedly and squeezed out a splodge of paint onto a paper plate, then dipped the brush in it. She was confident she'd read her client right too, and that he'd like this more modern style, with its splashes of purple and orange, and the little dog's left ear disappearing off the edge of the canvas. I am so lucky to do what I love, she thought.

And that's when the phone rang. And that's when everything started to change.

'Hello,' she said, unable to mask the irritation in her voice.

'Hello.' A woman's voice, hesitant. 'Is that Jenny?'

'Yes, speaking...'

'It's Claire.'

'Claire. Um.... Hi!' Jenny racked her brains. Claire, Claire. Did she know a Claire? Was it one of the school mums? Or that new girl from the book club?

'I know this is a bit out of the blue. I hope I'm not disturbing you.'

'Claire! No, of course not.'

She recognised the voice now, but she was puzzled. This was truly unexpected. Claire had been her closest friend when she was young, but she hadn't seen her for at least fifteen years. The last time must have been at Claire's wedding, but they hadn't really talked then. These days their contact was limited to Christmas newsletters and the odd bit of gossip passed on from their parents. Oh God, Claire's parents! If Claire was phoning her now, something must have happened to her mum or dad. She braced herself; they had been a lovely couple, a kind of second family, and she'd spent many happy holidays with them, camping in the Dales or the Lake District.

'Wow, this is a surprise. How nice to hear from you! How are you, Claire?' she asked now, hoping for the best.

'Oh, I'm good. How about you? How are the boys?'

'Oh, they're great. Well, they're bloody hard work to be honest, but they're great.' She remembered that Claire didn't have kids, so asked about her husband instead. 'How's Mike?'

'Erm... he's OK, I think.'

That's very odd, thought Jenny. She doesn't know. Maybe they're not together any more.

'So, what brings you back into contact? I mean, it's great to hear from you...'

'I know, I know. It has been a while. Well...' There was

a pause. 'It's hard to explain. It's going to sound crazy...' She sighed, then continued: 'What do you remember about that time I came to visit you at your parents' house, when we were about ten or eleven?'

'Which time? You came loads of times.'

'The time you taught me how to ride a bike. It would have been around 1990, or maybe 1989. It was a summer visit.

'Erm, I don't remember an awful lot, really. I remember we had fun. Why do you ask?'

'Do you remember that old house, the one we used to call the Scooby-Doo house?'

'Vaguely. Yes, yes, I think so. Why do you ask?' she said again.

'I think we witnessed a murder there.'

***

'She said *what?*' She had his full attention now. At last.

Paul had come in late, after eight o'clock. The boys were out of the bath and were in pyjamas, playing in their big shared bedroom. Paul had gone upstairs to read a chapter of Harry Potter before coming down, a satisfied smile on his face, and pouring them both a glass of wine.

That's it, he thinks he's father of the year 'cos he's read a bit of Harry Potter, thought Jenny, sourly, as he'd collapsed onto the red leather sofa and started flicking through the TV channels.

'What's for dinner?' he'd asked.

She'd started telling him about the phone call, but she could tell he was not really listening.

'I said I had a phone call from an old friend today.'

'Uh-huh' he said, pressing the recordings button on the remote and scrolling through the list of programmes.

'I hadn't seen her in years, it was really strange.'

'That's nice.' His voice was placating, vague. She decided to cut to the chase:

'She said she thought we'd witnessed a murder when we were young.'

'She said *what?*' At last he put the remote down and looked at her. 'Hang on, start again. Who is this woman? Do I know her?'

'She's Claire Hastings. She's one of my oldest friends. Our parents were at university together, so I've known her since we were born, really. But we got to be best friends when we were about nine or ten. We used to go and stay with each other more or less every holiday. You met her at our wedding.'

'Did I? I don't remember. So she just came out and told you that, just like that?'

'Yup.'

'What did you say?'

'I said I had no idea what she was talking about!'

'You don't remember anything happening?'

'No, not a thing.'

'Well, did she explain what she meant?'

'No, that's the strange thing. She wouldn't tell me more. She said she didn't want to influence me. She wanted me to try and remember on my own, to corroborate her. She asked me just to think about it.'

'But didn't she give you any clues?'

'Yeah, just one; she said it happened in this spooky old house we used to play in. But I can't remember anything.'

'Well, she must be a fruitcake. A nutjob. Where's the wedding album? Is she in it? Can you show me her photo?'

Jenny went to the bookshelves and fetched down a heavy album with a rather tacky embossed white plastic cover. She started turning over the stiff cardboard pages. Here was Paul, standing next to his best friend and best man, Joe. He looked unbelievably handsome in his dark green tartan kilt. He hasn't changed much since then, she thought. His sandy hair was still as thick, his body still taut and muscled. On the next page she saw herself, surrounded by her three bridesmaids. She regretted the dress a bit now; it was sleeveless, the boddice fitted tightly to the waist, but then the material flared out extravagantly in multiple folds to the floor. Bouffant styles had been all the rage at the time, but in retrospect she wished she'd chosen something slim and slinky. Paul's kilt would never date, but her dress screamed the early two thousands. She turned another page and saw the two of them together, at the church door. How young they both looked, gazing confidently into each other's eyes. They had been barely past the student years, full of optimism, ideology and principle. Both with decent jobs, determined to be a modern couple, to share chores, responsibilities and opportunities equally. Something's gone a bit awry there, she thought. I've somehow let myself fall in to the supporting role. How did that happen? Next, a photo with Paul's parents; Paul's father, Douglas, showing that a kilt could look just as good on a fuller figure, and his French mother, Chantal, looking – well, very French, in a well-cut cream suit. A few pages further on, she stopped and pointed. She and Paul were at the centre of the group. On the left were her parents, in their best wedding outfits, stiff and self-conscious, but beaming. On the left were Ken and Dora Hastings, smiling happily at the camera. And next to them, their daughter Claire. She was small and slim with fine, blow-away fair hair and freckles. She was wearing a long, flowing multi-coloured summer dress. Her eyes were big, blue and innocent-looking.

'She looks like a real hippy type. All whimsical and fey. I bet she's into mysticism and tree-hugging and all that crap. Like

I said, a nutjob.'

'No, not at all,' said Jenny, irritated by his quick dismissal. 'That dress makes her look a bit hippy-ish, but she's actually really down to earth. She's an accountant – you can't get much more sensible than that!'

'Huh,' Paul snorted, 'I've met a few accountants that would make your hair stand on end. But how did you leave things with her?'

'She said she'd phone me again in about a week, see if I'd remembered anything.'

'Well, my advice is to forget all about it. It can't be true. Seeing a murder is not the sort of thing you'd forget. She's 'mis-remembered' as Donald Trump might say.' He stretched and yawned, leaning back further into the sofa. 'So what *is* for dinner?'

***

Jenny lay in bed that evening, listening to Paul's gentle snores and trying to empty her mind and let sleep in. Tomorrow was a busy day. She had to get the boys off to school, then drive over the moors to visit a new client and take photos of her beloved cat for a portrait. Then back in time to make a cake or biscuits for the book club – it was at her house this time. Then a bit more painting, pick up the boys.... Karate after school tomorrow. Oh, shit! Did she need to clean their kit? The boys had been prac- ticing throws in the garden, she'd need to get the grass stains out. The list went on. She needed to get a full eight hours sleep, but her mind kept coming back to the phone call.

Claire. She hadn't really thought of Claire in a long time, and wondered why. They had been inseparable at one time, the firmest of friends. Jenny had put Claire on a pedestal that none of her schoolfriends could ever hope to reach. It had been a kind of infatuation; they wrote each other's names all over their pencil cases and in the margins of their school books, covered in hearts. They scratched their wrists till they bled and held them together to become blood sisters. She remembered the long months between visits, when she'd wait every day for the postman to come, and the intense joy she felt when a fat letter in loopy turquoise handwriting dropped onto the mat. She'd devour every word, reading some parts over and over, then rush off to her bedroom to start a reply. They never phoned; both sets of parents thought a phone call was an unnecessary expense when a letter would do. And the letters were so much more satisfying. They shared ideas on books, TV programmes, films. They invented pretend families and wrote each other rambling stories about each member. Jenny smiled at the memory. Her imaginary family had included cute little baby sister Rose, and wicked older sister Josephine, who was always getting into trouble. How come she could remember that so well, able to visualise the drawings she used to make of them, even down to Josephine's ugly glasses and straight brown hair? She had a good memory, surely. If she could remember that, then for God's sake, she could not have forgotten a murder!

When had they stopped being so close? They had written to each other religiously for five or six years, but the letters had started to come more and more infrequently as they approached the teenage years. Jenny had developed an interest in boys, had joined a local youth club and gone youth hostelling in the holidays with a big mixed group. Gradually she'd stopped asking her parents if Claire could come and stay. She wondered, now, if Claire had been hurt by that? Had she been cruel? Or had it been a natural progression for both of them? Part of growing up?

When she first got to university, Jenny had gone through a wild phase, drinking, partying, occasionally taking soft drugs. She remembered the only weekend that Claire had come to visit her in that first year. She'd been excited to see her friend again and looking forward to a good catch-up, but the visit had been awkward, strained. Jenny knew that she herself had changed since she'd left home; she felt unconstrained, liberated by university life, and had been experimenting with extreme haircuts, punk outfits and gothic eye make-up. She'd waited on the station platform in torn skinny jeans and Doc Martens, her hair shaved close on one side and long and messy on top. When Claire had stepped off the train in her neat skirt and blouse, undoubtedly beautiful, but in a very safe, classical way, Jenny felt just a tinge disappointed. After so many years of fearing being left behind by her slightly older friend, Jenny now felt that she was the one who had stepped ahead. They had tried to find a reconnection that weekend, but Claire didn't seem interested in drinking in the students' union, or going to an off-site party. She hadn't been quite able to mask her shock to see Jenny smoking. Trying to find common ground, they talked about their university courses, but with Claire doing maths and physics, and Jenny geography, there was little to say. If she was honest with herself, it had been a relief when Jenny had walked Claire down to the station on the Sunday evening. We've grown apart, she thought, making her way back to the campus. People do.

After that, there had been little direct contact. Their parents were still close though, so Jenny always knew more or less what Claire was doing. She'd heard she'd got a first class degree, and was now studying for accountancy exams. Had she been a bit snooty about Claire's chosen career, buying into the theory that accountancy was for the unimaginative? A few years later, she'd invited Claire to her wedding and was delighted to see her there. They'd kissed and chatted briefly. A couple of years further on, she and Paul had attended Claire's wedding, herself heavily pregnant. Claire had looked exquisite, her slim form encased in a fitted lace wedding dress, little pearls threaded into her pale blonde hair, while Jenny felt like an elephant in her unattractive green maternity dress. On that day she'd felt oceans apart from her oldest friend. That must have been the last time they'd seen each other. And since then, only snippets of news from the parents.

Jenny kicked herself now for not trying harder. She saw now that her wild student years had been a hugely enjoyable but brief flash in the pan; basically she was quite a conventional person. Had she written Claire off for being too conformist, letting the friendship slide, when in fact they were fundamentally very similar? What a waste! And later, when Jake and Davie were young, she had naturally gravitated towards other young working mums, instantly finding common ground in moaning about sleepless nights, picky eaters and the impossibility of fitting childcare around busy work schedules. In her mind's eye, Claire had become the pristine smart-suited, briefcase-carrying professional. The gulf had seemed unbreachable.

Now Claire was coming back into her life with a story of murder, and she didn't know how to react. It didn't fit with the mental image she'd held for so long. Did she really know her friend? What had happened in those intervening years? Maybe Claire was a different person now, more emotional, irrational. Murder! It couldn't be true, could it? She remembered only good times.

Her thoughts reached further back to all the wonderful holidays she'd spent with the Hastings family; the unbelievable freedom of sharing a tent while Claire's mum and dad slept in the caravan beside it. Climbing mountains in the Lake District, fetching warm milk from the farm in the Dales, damming peaty brown rivers and collecting stones that glittered with schist. All those memories were suffused with the scent of freedom, adventure, lightness and harmony. No dark clouds there.

She searched her memory for images of Claire's visits to her own childhood house, the house her parents still lived in now; Victorian, detached, semi-shabby, with its wrap-around garden and host of secret places. They used to escape to her bedroom for hours and hours, talking and laughing, recording songs from the radio onto an ancient tape player, recording their own voices and inventing silly jokes. They used to lock themselves in the bathroom and create potions by mixing shampoo, toothpaste, scent and anything else they could find into an old toothbrush holder, like junior alchemists. They stole chocolates from the cupboard and ran behind the shed to devour the whole block. All happy, happy memories of complicity, naughtiness and hysterical laughter. Nothing frightening had marred that time, she was sure.

She tried to pinpoint the year Claire had talked about. 1989 or 1990. She could remember teaching Claire to ride her bike, going up and down the back lane endlessly, shouting instructions as Claire wobbled and panicked. Then the unbelievable moment when her parents had actually agreed they could cycle outside on real roads. And yes, she remembered them cycling to the Scooby-Doo house, squeezing through the railings, drunk with excitement, looking for adventure and a mystery to solve. She tried and tried to remember the house itself. In vain. In her mind's eye it was inextricably linked to the house in the animated TV series: dark blue against a black sky, turreted, and with bats flying from the single lit window. That couldn't be right. Why couldn't she remember the house itself? Could it be possible she'd blocked out some awful memory?

2

Summer 1990

'A watched pot never boils, Jenny! They won't get here any faster if you keep looking out the window!'

'I know, Mum. But when do you think they *could* get here?'

'It might be in an hour, it all depends on the traffic. Come and help me make up the bed for Claire.'

'Oh, OK.'

Jenny trailed up the stairs reluctantly. But ten minutes later she was at her post again, looking out of the big bay window, her heart thumping every time a white car rounded the bend, but sinking again each time it passed without stopping. At last a white car did stop, right outside the gate. The passenger door opened and there was Claire's mum, Dora, looking very smart in a blue twin set and smoothing down her tweed skirt. Now the driver's door opened. Ken stepped out, his long face lined and kindly. He reached into his jacket pocket for his pipe, which he lit and sucked upon, looking up towards their house with a languid smile. And finally the back door opened. Two thin legs appeared first, clad in red sandals. Jenny made an immediate note to ask her mum for red sandals. And there at last was the whole of Claire, a skinny girl with wispy blonde hair, enormous blue eyes and a startled expression, as if she'd just been sleeping.

'They're here, they're here!' Jenny yelled, and bolted out

of the door and down the small flight of stone steps to the gate. As Claire's parents were getting a small suitcase out of the boot, she flung open the gate, then took a few paces back. Claire walked through. Then the two girls stopped, a couple of metres apart, suddenly shy and awkward. It was always like this. Months of letter writing, sharing intimate thoughts and declaring their passionate adoration of each other – writing 'I can't WAIT to see you' followed by a hundred exclamation marks – and now they were struck dumb, embarrassed. Claire was rubbing one foot against the back of the other ankle, looking anything but happy, and Jenny was suddenly panic struck. What if she doesn't want to be here? What if her mum and dad made her come? Maybe she's grown out of me and my stupid pretend family!

'Come on in! The kettle's on!' called Jenny's mum from the front door and the adults all went into the house, leaving the two girls frozen like statues by the gate. They gazed at each other. Jenny twisted her hair round her finger nervously and Claire looked solemn.

'Do you want to come up to my room?' asked Jenny at last.

And that's all it took. The spell was broken. They galloped up the stairs and threw themselves on the bed, both talking at once, then laughing. The relief of finding each other again turned to hysterics and they bounced on the bed until a sharp 'Stop that, you two!' came from downstairs. 'It's tea time. Come down now please, and fetch your brother too.'

***

Later that day, after Claire's parents had said goodbye, they both lay on their stomachs across the bed, heads together, looking at Jenny's bookshelves.

'What's your favourite Roald Dahl?' asked Claire.

'Matilda. What's yours?'

'The BFG. Have you read The Worst Witch?'

'No, is it good?'

'Yeah, it's OK. But my favourite is still Enid Blyton.'

'Me too! But I have to read them in secret. My mum says they're not good.'

'Why not?'

'I don't know. No idea. I think she said they're too sexy. No, sexist. Something like that. But I don't care. I think they're great!'

'Me too. Who do you like best, George or Anne?'

'George of course! Anne just does the boring stuff all the time, like cleaning and cooking. I'd hate to be her!'

'Me too. Shall we play Famous Five?'

'OK. Bags me George!'

'That's not fair, I want to be George!'

'We can both be George.'

'OK. We need a mystery to solve. Are there any secret places in the house? Do you ever go into the attic?'

'No, I'm not allowed, it's not safe. But the shed's full of spooky stuff the last people left behind, though. Or... I know! We could spy on the neighbours. I think they're up to something. There's a lot of banging going on in their house, and the husband looks weird.'

'Let's look in the shed.'

They ran down the stairs, along the Victorian blue and gold-tiled hallway to the back door, and out into the garden. Jenny removed the padlock from the cracked wooden door - it was never locked - and they peered inside the damp, gloomy space. Discarded tins and jars lined the shelves. Old wooden cabinets stood against one wall, their drawers stiff and swollen with damp and disuse. Cobwebs reached from the roof to every surface and they batted them out of their hair. Adjusting their eyes to the dim light, they began pull open the cupboard doors and drawers, examining and rejecting corroded batteries, broken torches, boxes and boxes of nails and screws, cracked vases and musty rolls of wallpaper. They turned again to the jars. They hung under the shelves, their lids having been cleverly screwed onto the underside of each shelf so they could not be spilled. The contents were cloudy, mysteriously unlabelled. Murky greenish and rusty brown liquids fired their curiosity. Claire attempted to unscrew one jar, with no success.

'I bet these jars are full of poison! Maybe the previous owners were poisoners.'

'Yes, yes, they could be! My Dad says the house belonged to a doctor before us. I bet he killed all his patients.'

'And buried them in the garden!'

'Yes, yes! The garden was a terrible mess when we bought the house. It was all dug up!'

They looked at an old wooden sledge in the corner, and a selection of broken tennis rackets and rusty golf clubs. Then Jenny's attention was caught by the two bikes beside the door, the only objects that looked in reasonably good condition, apart from the shiny gardening tools. She had an idea.

'Can you ride a bike yet?' she asked Claire.

'Not really. I'm not very good. Our road's too busy to practice on. My mum doesn't want me to go out.'

'I can teach you! It's safe round here! Then we can go off together and find a proper mystery. I'll borrow John's bike. We can take picnics and search for buried treasure and stuff.'

'Will your mum and dad let us do that?'

'Well...' Jenny was doubtful. 'We might have to lie a bit. We could tell them we're just going to the playground. They'll be OK with that.'

'OK. But where can we go to find a real adventure?'

Jenny thought for a long moment, then her face lit up with excitement. 'I know! There's a place I went to once with my brother John. It's really creepy. It's this big old house but it's all boarded up and the garden is all overgrown. It's like the house in Scooby-Doo. You're not supposed to go there. The gate is chained up and there's a sign that says 'Keep out' or 'Trespassers will be shot' or something, but there's a gap in the railings you can get through. We could go there?'

'Yes, yes!' Claire's eyes shone. 'Brilliant! If it's been abandoned there's bound to be a mystery to solve. We'll need a mystery solving kit. Have you got any binoculars? We'll need note book. Erm... what else?'

'Torch. Penknife. Let's see if any of these old torches work. There was a penknife in that second drawer, too. Dad's got binoculars. Let's get all that stuff together now. We can start practicing on the bikes tomorrow.'

Their faces were alight with anticipation as they made their way back to the house.

***

For the next two days, Claire wobbled up and down the back lane, with Jenny running after and shouting encouragement. Then on the third day they were ready. They went searching for a mystery.

And they found a lot more than their young minds could possibly cope with.

3

Jenny opened the door with an uncertain smile. She was nervous about this meeting. She had no idea what to expect, and didn't like to feel unbalanced. She'd spent the morning cleaning the house and making a cake, as if the queen were visiting. She'd tried on different outfits, unsure what impression she wanted to make. Stupid really. She'd said nothing to Paul, as he'd left for work. She didn't want to face his disapproval.

'Hello, Claire' she said.

'Hello.'

As soon as Claire spoke, Jenny felt a wave break inside her, and a rush of affection that brought tears to her eyes and made her voice wobble.

'Come in! Come in! Let's go through and sit in the kitchen.'

She took in Claire's appearance as she preceded her down the honey-coloured tiled hallway and into the kitchen. She had always been slim, but now she seemed more than a shade too thin. Her blonde hair was as pale as winter sunshine, caught up at the back of her head with a clip, but her eyes were tired and shadowed. She was wearing jeans and a beautiful sage green leather jacket and Jenny laughed at herself for instantly itching to own the same one.

'Have a seat. Tea or coffee?'

'Oh, tea please. Thanks. Your house is beautiful!' Claire was, in fact, rather intimidated by the stark minimalism of the kitchen. It looked a little too perfect, as if she'd wandered into a showroom instead of a family home. 'And those must be your boys?' she asked, moving into the more homely dining area and looking at the jumbled collection of photos fastened onto a corkboard with drawing pins.

'Yes.' Jenny went over to join her. 'That's Davie. And that's Jake in his karate kit.'

'They look like real characters. You're so lucky!'

'Yes, I am. Thanks,' said Jenny awkwardly, aware from what her parents had told her that Claire had had trouble conceiving.

'And Paul? What does he do now?'

'Huh! Good question. You know, I'm not really sure. He's just started his own business and it's to do with data security and cybersecurity. He keeps trying to explain it to me, but he uses words like contextual intelligence, glitch sourcing and vulnerability testing, and it all just goes way over my head. Day-to-day I have no idea what he actually does!'

'Does he work from home?' asked Claire, looking around a little anxiously, as if she half expected him to appear behind her.

'He used to, until last year. Now he's got office space and even an employee!'

'Wow! Impressive!'

Jenny was about to give her standard reply, how proud she was of her go-getting husband, but then she changed her mind. This was Claire, who she used to share everything with. She wanted to be totally honest.

'It *is* impressive, he's doing really well, but the truth is, I hardly see him these days. I probably shouldn't complain that he works so hard, but it makes life a pain for me. It's me who ends up doing everything in the house: the bills, the cleaning, fixing stuff, shopping. We promised we'd have a modern marriage and share stuff like that, but – well, he's never physically here. And he's missing so much of the boys growing up. He keeps saying 'be patient, things will get better' so.... Well, let's hope they do!' She shrugged. 'What about your husband, Mike? What does he do?'

Claire's slight smile disappeared and Jenny once again noticed the shadows under her eyes. She felt a surge of protectiveness. Claire took off her jacket, hung it over the back of a chair and sat down at the table. Jenny tried to hide her shock as she noticed how thin her friend's arms were; where there should have been muscle, the upper arms dipped inwards alarmingly. Was she ill? Could she be anorexic?

'It's a long story. Make the tea first, then I'll start from the beginning.'

Jenny placed two mugs on the table and sat down opposite Claire, waiting. As Claire started to speak, she nodded occasionally, but didn't interrupt.

'OK. We split up a year and a half ago. We started having problems when we were trying for a baby. We tried for years. We tried everything. Got tested. Tried IVF. Nothing worked. It put a strain on the marriage, of course, but I was expecting that. I'd read all the leaflets and joined the support groups. I was desperate to be a mother. More than him really. We didn't ever argue, but I secretly resented him for not caring as much as I did, for being too unsupportive. And I'm sure he blamed me. He thought I was overreacting, and that my stress was stopping me getting pregnant. I started to hate his mum, too; she was so tactless, always asking 'when am I going to be a grandmother?' I couldn't bear that! But he would never back me up and tell her to shut up. So after a bit we just ended up avoiding the subject. Babies became the elephant in the room. And then after a while he just started... to kind of... go off me. I suppose I wasn't much fun to live with, crying every month; or maybe it was only the baby idea which had kept us together. And if that wasn't going to work... So anyway, then I tried to change my own behaviour and be more positive and optimistic around him. I tried to win him back, to make allowances, but he got very distant. I told myself that he was perhaps just going through some kind of midlife crisis and I just needed to give him a bit of time. Maybe I should have shouted and yelled. Then we could have worked something out. Instead I was patient, understanding. I was waiting for him to open up, but he never did. I didn't handle it right. I don't know....

'Anyway, one day he just announced out of the blue that he couldn't do it anymore and he was leaving. I couldn't take it in. It was like a punch to the stomach. I pleaded, asked him to explain, asked him to give us another go. I said let's talk about adoption. I said I could come to terms with not having kids, if he could. I convinced myself I could have a perfectly satisfactory life by concentrating on my career. But he just refused to talk. He said that awful: 'it's not you, it's me'. And he left. So I held things together for a while, you know, I went through the classic stages of wanting answers, of denial, of anger. Eventually I came to terms with things a bit. We got a divorce, sold the house, I bought my little flat in Manchester. Financially it was OK, I had a good salary. I threw myself into the job, got a promotion. It was starting to get better. You know, it wasn't great, but it was do-able. I could see some hope around the corner. I even got to the stage of thinking I was better off without him. Then I found out he was with someone else. Much younger. Had probably been seeing her while we were still together. And she was pregnant. It's such a cliché isn't it? But it hurt. Oh, my God, did it hurt. I'd been kidding myself. I wanted a child more than anything on earth, and here he was, about to become a dad. It was so unfair.

'To cut a long story short, I had a breakdown. I just went to pieces. Couldn't work, couldn't think straight. Couldn't bear my own company. Couldn't cope with being alone. All the feelings that I thought I'd got rid of just came charging back again, ten times worse. I felt such a failure! And then I did something really stupid.'

Claire had been keeping her eyes down as she spoke, holding her tea mug in both hands and turning it slowly round and round. Now she glanced up at Jenny with an expression that was hard to read, half ashamed, half defiant. 'Something stupid' thought Jenny. What does that mean? Did she attack her ex-husband in some way? Take a sledgehammer to his car? Confront the girlfriend? Or does that mean she tried to kill herself?

'Anyway,' Claire continued, 'I ended up in a psychiatric hospital for six months. I was on really strong medication. They held my job open for me for a long as they could, but when I got out, I couldn't face going back. I'd lost all my confidence, so I quit. So here I am. I'm a mess. Out of work, divorced, seeing a psychotherapist every week, still on some pretty strong meds.'

'I'm so sorry!' said Jenny, inadequately. 'I had no idea. My parents never said anything.'

'No. Well, I think my mum and dad aren't comfortable talking about it.'

'All I can say is, he's an idiot! How could he leave you? You're amazing! He'll end up regretting it.'

'Maybe not. He'll have a kid after all.' She gave a short, rueful laugh, then looked up. 'Anyway, that's not why I got back in contact. I don't want you to feel sorry for me. I'm coping OK, really.'

Jenny reached across the table and gave Claire's hand a squeeze.

'So what's this got to do with when we were kids?'

'Well,' Claire paused and took a sip of her tea. Jenny noticed that her slender hands were shaking slightly. 'I get the impression my therapist thinks that most of my problems could be related to childhood issues. He hasn't exactly said so, but I can tell from the questions he asks. He seems to think that some traumatic experience in my past has influenced me, and that's why I've had relationship problems and anxiety attacks, and that's why I didn't cope with the split in a normal way. I thought it was all bollocks a first, still do really, but I had to go along with it. It's part of the deal, you have to pretend to take the therapy seriously, otherwise you end up back in the hospital. So I've had to play along, talk about my childhood, parents, friends, school, all that stuff. Anyway, you don't want to hear all the gory details. But basically, things have started coming back. I've started having flashbacks. To that summer holiday at your parents' house, I think it was in 1990. And I'm pretty sure we saw something terrible.'

'But what? What did we see? Tell me more!'

'We saw a murder.'

'How? What happened? I don't remember anything!'

'No, wait, I've thought this through. It would be a bad idea for me just to tell you. I don't want to put ideas in your head. Basically, I just want to know if I'm going mad or not, and if it really happened. Have you remembered anything at all?'

'I'm sorry. I've been trying and trying. Nothing's come back. I don't know what else I can do to help.'

'Well, I had one idea. I remember you kept a diary at that time. In fact I think my parents gave it to you one Christmas. You used to write it every night. Have you still got it?'

'Probably. Somewhere. God knows where... I'll try and find it.'

'That would be great, thanks. And maybe do you think you could ask your parents if they remember anything about that holiday? You know, maybe we acted strangely or had nightmares or something.'

'I'll ask. Of course I will. I really want to help.'

'That means so much to me! I can't thank you enough.' Claire sat back in her chair, relieved, exhausted. 'I've dropped a bit of a bombshell, haven't I?'

Jenny gave a short laugh. 'You can say that again. But Claire, listen. What do we do if it turns out it's true? What do we do then?'

'Take it to the police, I guess. There's no statute of limitations for murder.' She finished her tea, put the mug down and sat straighter in her chair. 'Now, let's talk about something else. I haven't seen you for so long. I want to see the rest of your house. It looks fantastic from what I've seen so far. And I want to see some of your paintings, and I really want to know how your parents are!'

Jenny jumped up, eager to show Claire around the house. She was secretly very proud of her interior design ideas, but underplayed them deliberately now, aware that Claire had had to move to a small flat. Once upstairs, she felt desperately awkward and embarrassed as Claire lingered in the boys' bedroom, picking up and absently stroking one of Davie's cuddly elephants.

'Ugh, it's such a mess in here!' complained Jenny, as if trying to somehow make amends for having children. She picked up the sweatshirts and underpants strewn across the floor with an exaggerated grimace. Claire just smiled and replaced the elephant on the bed.

The tour ended with the spare room studio. Claire seemed genuinely interested in the different types of oils and acrylics, together with the bottles of white spirit, gesso, linseed oil, thinner and varnish that lined the shelves.

'So, are you a full time artist now?' she asked, gazing at the Jack Russel on the easel.

'Um, well, that was the idea. I gave up my job with the town council when we moved up north. I'd been painting as a hobby for ages, and thought I might give it a go professionally instead of looking for another planning job. Paul was very encouraging. So, yes, I'm trying to make a proper career out of it.

If it doesn't take off I can always go back to town planning. But the trouble is, if you're in the house all the time, you get so side-tracked by all the stuff that needs doing. Cleaning, shopping, gardening - the boring stuff, you know?'

'Hmm.' Claire was unconvinced. 'Well, there's things you can do to make more time. You should maybe get a cleaner. And do your shopping online. And get Paul to do the gardening at the weekend. Oh, sorry, I'm being too bossy! Just ignore me.'

'No, you're absolutely right,' said Jenny. 'I guess I'm still having trouble thinking of it as a job, not a hobby. I still don't say 'I'm an artist' when people ask me what I do. It sounds so pretentious.'

'Well, you should! These are really good!'

'Um, thanks.'

When Claire left, an hour or so later, Jenny had mixed emotions. She was amazed at how easily they had talked, and how happy she felt to be in Claire's company again. She felt energised by Claire's praise of her paintings, and determined to push herself harder, be a bit more professional and ruthless in her work ethic. But when she remembered Claire's description of her time in the psychiatric hospital, that ambiguous sentence 'I did something stupid', the talk of medication and therapy, she couldn't suppress another, darker thought: was Claire mentally stable?

***

Paul got home late once again. His dinner would have to be microwaved once more, thought Jenny, annoyed. How long is it since we actually ate at the table together? But as he pushed off his shoes and collapsed on the sofa with a sigh, running his hands through his thick sandy hair, she felt an unaccustomed stab of compassion. He looked tired, washed out. He does work hard, I should give him a bit more credit, she thought. She dithered about whether or not to tell him about Claire's visit, but in the end needed to get it all off her chest. Paul's reaction was predictable.

'There you have it! What did I tell you? It's obvious. She's just out of the loony bin. She's maybe psychotic, probably delusional. She's taking drugs. She's trying to tangle you up in her delusions. Well, Jen, I don't think you should get involved in all that. We've got enough on our plate right now with the start-up. We don't have time for all that nonsense. Just tell her to fuck off. Nicely. You don't want her to do herself in.' He paused, then added, a little cruelly: 'Again.' He picked up the newspaper, signalling the conversation was closed, but Jenny was annoyed. She had had similar doubts herself, but now leapt to Claire's defence.

'Paul, don't be a prick! It's not really up to you to tell me what to do! I can make my own decisions. Anyway, she was quite composed and rational. As for being in the hospital, everyone has a breaking point. It could happen to you or me, with the right triggers.'

Paul snorted. 'I don't believe that. Some people are just genetically more predisposed to get mental illnesses than others. Anyway, the whole murder thing's ridiculous. You must admit it. I'm not discussing it any more. I'm off to bed. Are you coming?'

'What about dinner?'

'I'm not hungry. Had a big lunch. Are you coming up?

'Yes, in a bit.'

Jenny fumed silently. She knew her husband. He wasn't concerned so much for her welfare, as worried that his comfortable routine would be disturbed, that the backup she uncomplainingly provided might be compromised. Damn him and his bloody job, she thought.

Instead of climbing the stairs, she went into the garage,

switched on the bare overhead bulb and looked at the stack of cardboard boxes that had been left untouched since they moved here, over three years ago. Hasty descriptions had been scribbled on the sides in marker pen. *Random kitchen items*, and *unwanted wedding presents* and *second best sheets and duvet covers*. Predictably, at the bottom was the box she was looking for. *Old school books etc* was scribbled across the side. Could it be in there? Laboriously she started restacking the heavy boxes until she got to that bottom one. She hauled it onto a low shelf, grabbed a Stanley knife and sliced open the jungle tape. Inside a host of memories lay waiting to assault her. There was her school hymn book, scrawled with the signatures and words of wisdom of her sixth-form friends. Class photos dating back years. She found herself on the first one, appalled by her pudding basin haircut. Here were her geography A-level revision notes. Why had she kept them? And, right at the bottom, a little yellow mock leather-covered notebook book with a three digit lock combination. Her five-year diary, from the ages of about ten to fifteen. She broke open the lock, turned to a random page and started to read.

4

Summer 1990

They got off their bikes and wheeled them up to the rusty metal gates. A sturdy chain kept them firmly held together. The enormous stone gateposts were almost invisible behind curtains of ivy, but they could still make out a majestic pair of lions atop each one, and further down, the faded blue sign:

PRIVATE PROPERTY.

KEEP OUT. NO TRESPASSING

Jenny looked at Claire, a bit nervously. Her palms were sweaty. Maybe this wasn't such a good idea. She'd felt much braver when she'd been here with John, three years her senior. Now she was the one calling the shots and she suddenly had cold feet.

'Shall we just go home? We've cycled quite a long way today. I've got a sore bum, have you? Let's go home via the park and eat our picnic there.'

'No! Come on, we're here now! Where's that gap in the railings? I want to see inside.'

'OK then,' she sighed. 'This way.'

Jenny admonished herself for being a wimp. She knew she had to do whatever it took to keep up with Claire, to keep the friendship rock solid. They wheeled their bikes along the road for fifty metres, until Jenny found the place. The black paint was flaking off the rusted railings, which were topped with vicious looking spikes, but here, two of the metal bars had been bent outwards slightly, leaving just enough space for a small body to squeeze through. Behind was a dense, impenetrable looking jungle of overgrown trees and shrubs.

'What shall we do with the bikes?'

'We'll chain them up further along, so no-one thinks we've gone through the gap.'

Once on the inside, they felt safer, protected from view by the trees, and they started to explore. A couple of metres into the wood they found broken bottles and the charred remains of a campfire. They decided this was not very mysterious, probably just local teenagers drinking illicit beers. Then a little further in, they came to a small clearing. Several blocks of blackened masonry lay scattered about. Some blocks had deeply engraved letters and numerals, still visible through the greeny-grey lichen. They traced the letters and jotted down their findings in a note book.

'Here's a date. 1767. And some letters. R I G... it looks like H... I can't see any more.'

'Do you think they're gravestones?'

'Yes! Yes, I'm sure they are.' Jenny knew the stones were in fact much too small, and had probably belonged to some old building that had fallen down. But they were here to find a mystery, so she improvised. 'They must be children's graves. What if the people in the house killed their children and buried them here where no-one would find them?'

'Yes! Of course! Let's see if we can make out more names on the stones.'

Next, deep inside the wood, they found the domed brick roof of a small building, buried into a slope and almost entirely hidden under a tangle of shrubs. An iron gate hung loosely from a broken hinge, covering the entrance. They pulled it, but it would not budge, the wild plants having tied it firmly in place. Behind the gate, they could make out a dark passage which seemed to lead downwards, and in front, piles of dry leaves had collected. Jenny knew exactly what this building was. An ice house, where in the old days, people used to cut ice from lakes and store it, to keep their food and drinks cold. Her dad had told her that when they visited a stately home once. But she wasn't going to tell Claire that. This was perfect mystery fodder.

'A secret house!' she said. 'This could be where they hid the treasure! It's got to be!'

'Yes! Yes! We've got to get the door open and explore. Where's the torch?'

Claire was rummaging about in the backpack impatiently, and once again Jenny was wrongfooted by her eagerness. 'She's much braver than me,' she thought.

'Erm… let's do that tomorrow. It's getting a bit late. Mum and Dad will be starting to wonder where we are. We'll eat our picnic here, then go back home and write everything up in the Mystery Book. We'll make a map of all the stuff we've found today.'

**

On the fourth day they got as far as the house. It was a hot day, the kind of perfect English summer weather that occurs too rarely. Jenny's mum had waved them off with egg sandwiches and crisps, making them promise to go no further than the park and be back by tea-time. With no trace of guilt, they cycled past the park and on for two or three further miles, until they reached the gap in the railings.

It was a welcome relief to escape the heat of the sun and lose themselves in the dark of the woods. They passed the graves once again. Then, as they'd approached the ice house, a pheasant had shot out from the undergrowth beneath their feet with a loud rustling, a flash of feathers and a sharp alarm call, startling them, making them scream in delighted terror, and sending them dashing full pelt through the wood. The light slapped into their eyes as the trees thinned. Finally out of breath, they stopped, laughing hysterically, their bare legs scratched and bleeding slightly.

'Oh God. I've got a stitch.'

'Me too. It was a bird!'

'I know!' Claire was bent double, holding her stomach. When at last she looked up, she gasped.

'Look!'

And there it was. Through a gap in the trees they could see the house and its setting.

What had once been formal gardens were now abandoned and wild. The stone walls enclosing the garden were blackened and crumbling and the hedges tall and shapeless. Moss-covered steps led to an area of lawn, now high with yellowing weeds. Two statues stood either side of the steps; one was male, nude, headless. The other was a woman. Ivy crawled up the torso and the face was streaked with black, giving it an unsettling tear-stained appearance. Yet more ivy twined around the back of the head, like green hair.

Cautiously, they walked up the steps, Jenny avoiding eye contact with the gruesome statue. Instead she looked ahead and to the left, and saw a small lake glistening still and silent. A rotten-looking wooden jetty stretched several metres into the water, and an old rowing boat was attached to the side. She felt a sudden chill and grabbed Claire's hand. Claire yelped in surprise, then they both giggled.

Together they made their way up the path, edging past an empty fountain, until the house stood before them. Another flight of wide, moss-covered steps led up to a heavy front door. The building rose three stories high. The bottom windows were boarded up, and covered in graffiti. The top ones were dark, some broken. Ivy climbed up the stone walls, reaching almost as high as the two turrets that stood at each corner. Despite the hot day, there was an atmosphere of dank and ruin here.

They walked up to the front door, and past the boarded up windows. Claire pulled at the lower boards to see if any were loose, but they held tight, to Jenny's relief. Then, following the wall around the corner, they saw what at one time must have been an impressive oval greenhouse, now just a tangle of metal and broken glass. Rampant greenery was pushing up what remained of the walls and through the skeletal ceiling. It was easy enough to get in; the door had long ago lost its glass. Inside was strangely beautiful, from the web of ivy covering the floor to the remains of the intricate domed ceiling. They began to explore, pulling at the ivy to discover the shapes of benches and seats underneath. Here were some rusted garden implements. And there a stack of clay plant pots, long-dead insects inside.

'Let's go back to the house, I don't think there's any mystery here,' said Claire after a while, turning towards the entrance.

'Hey, wait a minute,' said Jenny. 'There's something in this dirty old tin. It rattles.' She gave it a shake. Something substantial clonked against the sides. 'It could be some treasure!'

'Well, open it then!'

It looked like an ancient biscuit tin. There had once been a picture on the lid, but it was now covered in rust. The hinges were equally corroded and Jenny fought to get the tin open. She was on the point of giving up, when the lid snapped off completely and the contents fell to the floor.

Both girls stared down, mesmerised, incredulous. It lay on the ground, cushioned in ivy: a six inch piece of rough brown metal. The bow at the top was carved into the shape of a crown. The heavy shaft was decorated with two collars and the tip showed three indentations. Claire picked it up and looked at

Jenny, wide-eyed and solemn.

    'Bloody hell! I think you've found the key!'

5

'What's that you've got there?' asked Paul, surprising her. He dumped his work bag on the floor and came over to join her.

'Oh, hi! I didn't hear you come in!' Jenny closed the little book hastily. 'What time is it?'

'Quarter past eight, about.'

'How was work today?'

'Busy, as usual. I'm bloody knackered. So what were you reading?'

Jenny sighed. Paul was going to get on his high horse again, she was sure. 'It's my old diary. Very, very old. It's a five year one. It's crazy how much you change between the ages of ten and fifteen. From sweet little girl who loves her parents and does her homework, washes her hair once a week and looks forward to the next episode of Byker Grove, to nightmare teenager, uncommunicative and angry at the world.'

'What have you dug that out for? Is it to do with that woman?'

'You mean Claire?' said Jenny, annoyed. 'Well, yes. I promised to help her. I said I'd see if I'd written anything strange about that visit.'

'And…?'

'No, I haven't found anything yet. Not really. I think I've got the right year and the right holiday. But there's nothing frightening so far.'

'Read us out a bit.'

'Are you sure? I thought you said the whole murder thing was bollocks.'

'I do think it's bollocks. Maybe if you read it aloud you'll realise it's bollocks too.'

'OK then. Here goes… *Saturday 4 August: Claire is here! We made potions and got found out. Sunday 5 August: Claire can almost ride my bike. We're going to find a mystery. We ate banana sandwiches for lunch. Monday 6 August: We took the bikes to the park. Claire fell off and hurt her knee. We followed a man because he looked strange. Tuesday 7 August: We went to the Scooby-Doo house and found the graves. We have started the Mystery Book. John is being horrible. Wednesday 8 August: We found a key it's very old. John found the Mystery Book. I hate him. Thursday 9 August: We saw the caretaker and he shouted at us. I wish Claire wasn't leaving on Saturday.* And then it stops. There's nothing for the next three days. The next entry talks about being excited about going camping with Mum and Dad in France.'

'So the only vaguely scary thing is that someone shouted at you?'

'Yeah.'

'If you ask me, that proves nothing happened. It's all in her head.'

'But what about the missing three days? I never used to miss a day, and three in a row is odd.'

'It could be anything. Maybe you were sick, or just fed up. Listen Jen, I had a bit of time today. I was waiting for a client who never showed up. Anyway, I did some research about repressed memory and false memory.' Paul looked very pleased with himself. He fetched his reading glasses and his mobile from his bag and began to talk, earnestly. 'There are almost no proven cases of repressed memory, or dissociative amnesia as they call it. It doesn't really exist! They call it a 'pseudo-neurological condition.' People have believed for years that you block out a traumatic memory, but there's no scientific evidence for it at all, it's a kind of myth. Listen to this: I've got the text on my phone. Hang on a minute while I find it.' He scrolled through his Google search memory until he came to the right page. 'Blah, blah, blah... Here! Listen: *research cited by Otgaar, et al. suggests that between 40-89 percent of the general lay public believe that traumatic memories can be suppressed and forgotten, that even an act of murder can be suppressed. Events of our past may sometimes come back to us in sudden recollection. But research finds no evidence that this happens with traumatic memories. Indeed, prospective research (following people after a traumatic event) finds that though trauma victims would like to forget their experiences, they do not.* So you see, you can't just block out something like a murder.'

'OK' said Jenny, nodding slowly. 'Yes, I suppose you're right.'

'But here's the thing,' Paul was on a roll. 'False memory absolutely exists. You can very easily implant a memory in someone by suggesting something, and they really start to believe it actually happened. You said Claire was having therapy. Well, a shrink who believes he's treating a repressed memory can easily convince a patient that he experienced something that he did not. There's loads of cases of patients believing they were abused as kids, and even parents being jailed, and it turns out the therapist planted a false memory. Listen, there's another bit here that's interesting.' Again he scrolled through his Google searches. 'Here it is. It's talking about miscarriages of justice, when people are falsely accused of incest and stuff: *Typically such cases occur when a vulnerable individual seeks help from a psychotherapist for a commonly occurring psychological problem such as anxiety, depression, low self-esteem, and so on. At this stage, the client has no conscious memories of ever being the victim of childhood sexual abuse and is likely to firmly reject any suggestion of such abuse. To a particular sort of well-meaning psychotherapist, however, such denial is itself evidence that the abuse really did occur.'*

'You think that's what happened to Claire?'

'Well, would you say she's vulnerable, depressed, anxious?'

'Yes, I guess so.'

'Well, there you go. False memory. And Jen, the thing is, Claire could pass the false memory on to you. If she totally believes it, you could start to believe it too.'

'Don't be daft. I'm not depressed and vulnerable!'

'No, but you're really empathetic. You could sort of get inside her head, share her thoughts. You've got to be careful, that's all I'm saying. Don't get involved.'

Jenny snapped the little yellow diary shut and stood up. She smiled at Paul.

'Well, thanks for doing all that research. It's good to know the pitfalls. I'll be careful, I promise. I'll keep my head.'

'Do you mean you're still going to continue looking into the murder thing?'

'Yes, for a bit. I owe it to her, Paul. I want us to visit Mum and Dad at the weekend. See if they remember anything, and even if nothing comes of it, they'll love seeing the boys again.'

Paul looked momentarily angry. Then he sighed. 'You go, if you must. I haven't got the time. I need to work this weekend.' He stood up. 'Just don't come running to me if you find the whole thing's a complete waste of time. Right.' He slapped his thighs decisively. 'I'm going for a run.'

'What, now? It's almost dark! And I've made a curry.'

'Don't wait for me. I'll warm mine up when I get back.'

Jenny watched his retreating back, exasperated. He hates it when I don't automatically fall in with him, she thought. She pictured Claire's delicate, strained face and trembling hands once again, and knew that she'd do almost anything to help her.

I hope he doesn't make me choose between a friendship and my marriage, she thought.

6

Summer 1990

'The chain's not there anymore!' said Jenny.

'Oh yeah, you're right! What does that mean? Do you think someone's gone in?'

'I think they must have done. Look, you can see some marks on the other side.' She pointed at the two quarter-circles etched deeply into the gravel where the gates had been forced open.

Jenny was annoyed. This was their special place, and she didn't want anyone else to discover it. 'Do you still want to go in?'

'Yes of course! We'll go through the gap, though. And we'll be very careful. Have you got the key?'

'Yes, it's in my pocket.'

Cautiously, they made their way through the trees, past the little stone 'graves', past the ice house, and into the once formal garden. They paused and looked around for signs of life, but there was nothing. A light rain had started to fall. Ahead of them, the house stood silent. They could see no vehicles, nothing had changed. To their left, heavy clouds hung over the still, grey lake.

'There's no one here. Let's run to the house before we get wet. Race you!'

Giggling, they raced up the steps, past the statues and past the empty fountain, pulling at each other's clothes and elbowing each other to gain an advantage. Then they ran full pelt along the overgrown path. Almost neck and neck, Claire just reached the massive front door first, reaching her hand out to slap it and shouting 'I win!'

'You cheated! You set off before me! And you didn't say ready, steady, go!' Jenny complained, panting.

The house loomed above them, dark and gloomy against the lowering sky. Suddenly they were apprehensive, filled with the enormity of what they were about to do. Jenny felt the key, heavy in her hand. They looked at each other solemnly.

'Shall we really try it?'

'Well, we're here now,' said Claire. 'Anyway, I bet it's not even the right key. Let's try it and see.'

The key slid easily into the lock. They both held their breath as Jenny gripped the decorative crown-shaped bow and turned. Clunk!

'Crikey!'

'Oh bloody hell!' Jenny's heart was thudding against her rib cage. 'It works!'

It was Claire who finally gripped the doorknob and turned it. The door creaked open slowly, groaning against its rusty hinges.

'Crikey!' said Claire, again. 'That's the noise the doors always make in Scooby-Doo!'

They stared at each other for a moment, then collapsed into uncontrollable nervous giggles.

'Stop, I'm going to wet myself!'

'I think I just have done!'

Taking deep breaths, they braced themselves, pushed the door wide open and stepped inside. They found themselves in a dark, shadowy entrance hall. Pale sunlight filtered down from the windows in the floor above, casting meagre rays of light into the gloom. Dust motes swirled around in the light beams, released from their torpor by the sudden blast of fresh air. The filthy floor was scattered with old pieces of wood, stone and broken crockery. They could just make out the shape of the tiles below the grime. Something skittered away across the floor – a mouse perhaps. A once-grand sofa stood against the wall to their left, its faded covers ripped and spilling out entrails of what looked like straw. Opposite the door were two marble plinths, one holding a Greek-style bust, the other standing empty. To their right, a broad staircase littered with debris led to a balcony which spanned the entire first floor. And in the middle of the hall were two objects covered in dirty grey dustsheets.

They stared at each other in awe. It was all too much to take in, too real, too perfectly mysterious. Much more than they had bargained for.

'What do you think is under those sheets?' asked Claire.

'I don't want to know. This is too creepy. I... I don't want to be here anymore. I don't like it. I don't care about the mystery. Can we just get out of here?' She knew she was not being brave, but to her surprise, Claire agreed:

'Yep, I don't like it either! Let's go back to your house.'

Relieved, they ran outside, closing the heavy oak door behind them and leaning against it, panting, trying to slow their racing heartbeats. Then they walked slowly down the steps.

'*Oi!*' A man's voice, loud, close and angry, froze them to the spot. 'You kids! What the fuck are you doing here? This is private property. Come here, you little fuckers!'

Clutching each other in fear, they turned to see a powerfully built man in jeans and a stained white tee shirt striding towards them from the side of the house, his face puce with fury.

They ran.

'Fucking kids! How the fuck did you get in! If I ever catch you here again I'll...' The voice receded as they flew down the path and into the safety of the trees. In the clearing they stopped to catch their breath.

'Is he following us?'

'No, I don't think so. I can't hear anything.'

'God, that was close!'

Dizzy with relief and high on adrenalin, they threw themselves onto the grass in the clearing and started to speak, each sentence coming faster and faster.

'Who was that? Did you see his face? I thought he was going to kill us!'

'I know! And the way he was swearing! He's a bad man. He's got to be up to something.'

'Of course! Remember in Scooby-Doo? It's always the caretaker who's the baddy. He must be the caretaker!

'The Caretaker! Yes he must be! His clothes were all messy and dirty, he wasn't smart enough to be the owner.'

'And did you see his face? He had a scar over his eye! Like a boxer or a gangster or something!'

'And he was so tall. Taller than both our dads. And his hair – it was red and curly!'

'I bet he's hiding something in the house!'

'Or stealing something from it.'

'We've got to find out what he's up to.'

'We could stop him.'

Yeah.' Jenny put on a fake American accent: 'I would have got away with it, if it wasn't for those meddling kids.' They both laughed, slightly hysterically.

'Well, how do we find out what he's up to?'

'We'll do a stakeout, like they do in The Bill.'

'What's The Bill? What's a stakeout?'

'It's a TV programme about police. And it's when you hide and watch someone to catch them doing something. We'll come back tomorrow, hide in the woods and watch him with binoculars.'

'Is it safe? What if he catches us?'

'He won't catch us. Anyway, we can run faster than him.'

Jenny was drunk with the drama of their narrative. The real fear she had experienced minutes earlier was gone. This was a mystery of their very own. Something to bind the two of them ever closer together. Something, with a bit of imagination, that they could expand and add to over the next few months in their letters. This would be so much better than writing about pretend families! This was great! She had a feeling that Claire was growing out of the pretend families stage anyway. Getting bored with the stories. Or finding them too babyish. She was five months older, after all - maybe that made all the difference. Her letters had been getting shorter and shorter before this visit, and Jenny was terrified of being left behind. This changed things! Maybe Claire would come again at half term. They could invent a whole list of villainous characters by then. In her heart of hearts she knew that the man in jeans was probably just a workman, or a gardener, come to the house to start some repairs. But with their joint imaginations they could build this into something huge that would sustain and cement their friendship. She hugged her knees and beamed up at Claire.

'Come on! Let's go home and draw some pictures of the Caretaker and stick them in the Mystery Book. Then we'll plan for tomorrow. It's our last day together. We've got to find out as much as we can.'

***

They spent a happy evening sitting at the red Formica kitchen table, drawing, colouring and gluing, arguing about which side of his face the scar had been on, and whether he had been wearing boots or trainers. When John entered the kitchen they flung their arms protectively around the book and glared at him.

'What are you doing?'

'Nothing. It's none of your business.'

'Let's see what you've got there!'

'No! It's secret. Get lost, John.'

Watching him leave, Jenny felt a twinge of remorse. John was actually very decent, as older brothers go. He was patient and kind, and often included her in the group when his friends came over to play guitar. But Claire came first, and there was no way he could be let into their secret. They hid the Mystery Book carefully out of his reach and talked excitedly far into the night.

But the next day something happened that they would never dare to speak about - not for another thirty years.

7

'Are we nearly there yet?' Davie asked again from the back seat.

'Davie, you know we've only just got onto the motorway! There's another half-hour at least. I know, let's play Road Trip Bingo. Let's see… you need to find a blue car, a caravan, a car with a foreign number plate and a truck with a supermarket logo. Ready?'

'Aw, mum! That's so lame!' grumbled Jake. 'I don't know why we have to go to stupid Granny's house anyway. They haven't even got internet.'

'Jake! Don't be such a misery-guts. You know Granny cooks the best puddings. I bet there'll be treacle tart, or lemon meringue pie. And I know that Grandad has made something for you.'

'What? What is it?' asked Davie.

'It's a surprise. Wait and see.'

'I bet it's lame,' said Jake, under his breath.

Jenny struggled to stay calm as she overtook a high-sided lorry on the windy Pennine motorway. Her nerves had been frayed since she'd woken up that morning. Paul had pointedly refused to speak to her. He'd dressed silently and gone down to the kitchen. There hadn't been the usual Saturday morning cup of tea in bed. Instead she'd heard the door slam shut as he'd left for his office. Why is he so angry? she asked herself. Does he feel threatened by an old friendship? Is he that insecure? Does he resent me making decisions? Or maybe he's really stressed at work, and taking it out on me? She remembered Claire saying she wished she'd shouted and got things out into the open when her own marriage started to feel strange, instead of smoothing things over. She was damned if she'd make the same mistake. Paul was behaving like a spoilt idiot and she would tell him so!

The wind dropped as the car left the high moors and entered the outskirts of West Yorkshire's urban towns. Jenny started to relax as she passed all the landmarks she knew so well. There was the fish and chip shop on the corner. The pub with the nice beer garden. The church on the hill. At last they came to a stop outside the fine old Victorian house. The enormous cherry tree was in blossom and the front beds were a riot of tulips and daffodils. But Jenny also noticed the cracked paint on the door and window frames, and the moss growing on the path. The house is starting to look a bit worn-down, she thought. Mum and Dad are getting older, maybe too old to cope with such a big house. The thought squeezed her chest tight for a moment, but then the front door opened and there they were; her mother wiping her hands on a tea towel and her father stretching out his arms to welcome them. An immense sense of calm and well-being suffused Jenny, as the boys rushed past her towards her childhood home.

'Come in! Come in!' said her dad. 'My goodness, you boys have shot up again! I can't believe it! I can't pat you on the heads anymore! Come on into the living room.'

'How was the journey?' asked her mum, a worried half-smile on her face. 'Was it awful with this wind? I do wish Paul had been able to drive you here.' Jenny's mum had never learnt to drive. As a consequence, and due to her own rather sheltered upbringing, she thought driving was some incredibly difficult task best undertaken by men.

'Mum, it was fine! You mustn't worry,' said Jenny, pushing

down her irritation at her mother's old-fashioned ideas. 'I'm actually a much better driver than Paul, you know. He's too impatient.'

'Grandad, what's the surprise? Can we see it now?' asked Davie.

Her dad winked at Jenny. 'Go on then. Come with me. It's in the garden.'

'I'll put the kettle on, shall I?' said Jenny's mum, as they left the room. 'Grandad's made the boys a go-kart. He's been at it for weeks. I do hope they like it.'

'They'll love it! Oh, it's so nice to be here.'

Jenny kicked off her shoes and sank back in the old-fashioned plush armchair, while her mum went out to make the tea. The room had not changed a bit since she was a child. The same gold button-back three piece suite with the nail-head trim on the arms. The nest of tables – she'd seen the same thing on Bargain Hunt just last week. The bulky TV set on its heavy stand with its video cassette recorder underneath. Her parents hadn't progressed to DVDs, let alone Netflix. The bones of the room were very fine though, with intricate coving and a beautiful plaster rose on the ceiling. The double-doors through to the rarely used dining room had exquisite stained glass panels inset into the wood. But Jenny noticed with some dismay that the paintwork above the big bay window was streaked with reddish brown. Was the window letting in water? Yet another sign that the upkeep might be getting too much for them.

'Do you ever think about moving to a smaller place?' she asked, as her mother came in with a tray of tea and flap-jack. 'Something easier to maintain?'

'Oh no! It's such a wonderful house when everyone comes to visit at Christmas. There are enough rooms for all of you. And it's wonderful to see the children playing in the garden. I had hoped you or John would inherit this house one day and keep it in the family. I don't suppose John will, now, though.' She looked momentarily sad. John had recently moved to a small wooden chalet in a remote part of Orkney, about as different from this house as you could possibly get, with minimal furniture and an upkeep that was limited to a fresh coat of wood sealant every year. Her parents had been dumbfounded, but Jenny privately thought he had made a wise choice. Much as she loved this house, she'd hate to be responsible for looking after it.

'No, we'll not move now. You'll have to carry me out of here in a box!' her mum continued, pushing disappointment aside and regaining her cheerful demeanour.

That's a nice job that'll fall to me and John one day, thought Jenny. Sorting through decades of accumulated junk: several thousand books, hundreds of LPs, piles of old Country Life magazines, cupboards threatening to burst with so many packs of photos and boxes of slides. Her parents were of the generation who never threw away anything that might one day be useful. This had proved a godsend whenever the boys needed to make something for a school project; egg cartons, loo rolls, cornflakes boxes, string, ribbons, crumpled wrapping paper, old yoghurt pots – a trip back home would provide everything needed to build a model volcano or a medieval castle. Yes, one day someone would have to get to grips with all the clutter. But not for many years yet, Jenny hoped.

'So, tell me all the news!' said her mother. 'How are the boys getting on at school? And is Paul getting lots of new business?'

Jenny put a positive spin on events, not wanting to worry her mother with news of Jake being called into the headmaster's office for fighting, or Paul spending less and less time at home. She had a close, loving relationship with her mother, but Jenny was aware that her role was to be positive and upbeat, and to provide lots of ammunition that her mum could throw out casually at her coffee mornings. She felt a bit miffed that her mother never asked how her own work was going. I work too, you know, she wanted to shout. But shouting had never been a part of how this family communicated.

After a while, Jenny brought up the main reason for her visit. 'Mum, I had a real surprise the other day. Guess who came to visit? Claire!'

'Claire? Oh, how lovely! You two used to be such close friends. I remember your two little blonde heads almost touching while you drew at the kitchen table. You were like two peas in a pod. How is she?'

'Oh, well, she's actually split up with her husband, Mike, which is a bit sad. But she's got a lovely little flat in Manchester and is doing OK. We talked a lot about old times and how much she loved coming to stay in this house.'

'Yes, all those visits, over the years! You two used to disappear for hours on end. Parents wouldn't let their children do that now, would they? People are too worried about paedophiles.' She paused, thinking. 'Do you think we were a bit irresponsible as parents?'

'Oh, God no, don't be daft, it was a brilliant childhood. You've got to give kids freedom to scrape their knees and fall out of trees – within limits. Did you know we used to cycle as far as that big old house down the Barnsley road?'

'Which house do you mean?'

'It was an abandoned house, kind of a stately home, you know, up past the field with all the horses.'

'You don't mean Blackmere Hall do you? That's miles away! I'd never have let you go so far!'

'Um… well… we didn't exactly tell you. But yeah. We used to crawl through the railings and play in the woods there.'

'Well I never! You little monkeys!'

'So you never knew?'

'I certainly did not!'

'Whatever happened to that house? It was in a really bad state back then. Really overgrown and covered in graffiti. Did they pull it down or convert it into flats?'

'Oh no! You should see it now! It's a really smart country club hotel type place, with a spa and everything. People have their wedding receptions there. They do conferences as well. They've got a very good restaurant too – I went for a meal there last year with Sheena from next-door.'

'Goodness! I can't imagine! It must have taken years to restore. Who bought it?'

'Oh, you know, that big-wig. Um, what's his name, now? He's a big businessman, he owns lots of hotels all over Yorkshire. He's on the arts committee with your dad, too. He's chairman. Oh, it's on the tip of my tongue... Begins with a 'T'. Honestly, my memory these days... Oh wait, it'll be in the art committee newsletter.' She pushed herself with difficulty out of the chair, went over to the antique roll-top writing desk in the corner and began to rummage through the stack of old bills, money-off offers and circulars which were stuffed there out of the way.

'Ah, here it is.' She held up a slim white magazine triumphantly. 'Let's see now. That's it. Tommy Whitaker. That's the chap.'

Jenny reached out and took the magazine, open at the page listing committee members. The name meant nothing to her.

'He's running for election on the city council too. Your Dad doesn't like him very much. He says he knows bugger all about art.' She gave a little laugh, her hand over her mouth, feigning embarrassment at having repeated a swear word. But her eyes had a wicked sparkle. Jenny knew she loved dropping in a good swear word now and again.

Jenny flicked through the magazine idly. The various

cultural events of the past month were described in glowing terms. Family days, creative workshops at the museum, school projects and new exhibits. Most of the photos were black and white, and did not do much justice to the art on display. However, the middle pages were given over to a full colour photo. A tall, heavily-built man was standing next to a Barbara Hepworth sculpture, his hand resting possessively on the smooth surface. He was smiling, but there was something odd about his eyes. Or maybe it was just the scar that ran from one eyebrow to cheek, giving his expression a disjointed look. Both eyes sending a different message. His hair was receding and greying but still curly, with just a hint of ginger. She read the caption below the photo:

Tommy Whitaker proudly shows off a fine Barbara Hepworth sculpture, on loan for the season to Blackmere Hall Hotel and Country Club.

Behind the man, manicured lawns stretched down to a lake with a little wooden jetty. Something began to stir in Jenny's brain. She felt suddenly cold and sweaty, all at the same time. It was not so much the man, but the jetty. There was something familiar about that jetty, something… almost evil.

'Can I borrow this?' she asked.

'Yes, of course, dear,' said her mum. 'Now, did I tell you about Sheena's daughter, Moira? She's been having a bit of a hard time recently. She found a lump and thought she might have breast cancer and…'

Jenny listened with half an ear as her mother gossiped about someone she'd never met. She felt a bit sick, dizzy. Why the hell had that photo given her such a strange reaction?

***

Lunch was superb, as usual. Jenny helped with the washing up, once again fruitlessly trying to persuade her mother to accept the benefits of a dishwasher. Then, with the plates and pots all stacked neatly away, Jenny and her dad put on their coats and joined the boys outside. Together they walked up the steep lane behind the house, to reach the grassy fields at the top. Jenny took a moment to look back, admiring the skyline of the industrial town. The cathedral, the town hall, several smaller churches and even the three tall blocks of flats – they all looked softer and almost romantic in the pinkish light of the afternoon.

As Jake and Davie took turns to plod up to the top of the field, then career down on the go-kart, Jenny stood at the bottom, her head resting lightly on her dad's shoulder. She adored her father. She loved her mother too, but the teenage years had been fraught, with many an argument and long periods of silent moodiness. 'You treat this house like a hotel!' had been a constant complaint. Her dad had been the voice of calm and reason, the conduit of communication between herself and her mother when they were no longer speaking. He was a deeply intelligent man, but modest and self-effacing, with a gentle wry humour.

'Mum was telling me about Blackmere Hall, earlier,' she said now, hoping her dad could provide more insight into the place. 'Apparently it's quite posh these days.'

'Yes, so I believe. I haven't been there myself. It's not really my cup of tea.'

'And she said the guy that owns it is on the arts committee with you.'

'He is, yes. Mr Whitaker.'

'What's he like?'

Jenny saw her dad frown and guessed he was struggling to find the right words. He genuinely tried to see the best in everyone, and rarely criticized, but it was obvious he didn't particularly like this man.

'Well, he's a typical committee man, I suppose you might

say. He loves the limelight. He's happy to talk to the press and give speeches at functions. And he's very good at that. He's good at fundraising, too. But between you and me, I don't think he actually likes art very much. I doubt if he'd know a Picasso from a Rembrandt.'

Jenny smiled. She could imagine it only too well, her dad doing a lot of the leg-work in his quiet, unassuming way, and this man stepping in when the hard work was done, accepting all the credit.

'You should be the chairman, Dad,' she said.

'Oh, no, I'm quite happy being the envelope-stuffer!' he replied with a laugh.

***

It was after seven in the evening when they finally left the house, her mum having pressed them to stay for soup, sandwiches and chocolate cake. Jenny hugged her parents hard on the doorstep, a lump in her throat. She always hated this moment. They were only in their mid- to late-seventies, but some tiny insistent voice inside her head whispered that she might never see them again. Don't be daft, she told herself. Seventy-five and seventy-eight is young these days!

Driving back over the moors in the early evening, with the boys unusually quiet in the back, Jenny thought about her father. He's almost exactly the opposite of Paul, she mused. Dad is quiet and patient and tolerant, whereas Paul is energetic, impatient and opinionated. Did I go all out to choose someone different? To break away from the gentle, slightly stuffy mould of my childhood and find someone who'd shake things up? She hoped Paul would be in a better mood when she got home.

But, of course, as soon as she opened the front door, she saw the lights weren't on.

He wasn't back.

8

'So, shall I pretend to be getting married, or you?' asked Claire, looking ahead at the road. Her pale hair was tied back severely, and Jenny thought that, plus the black round-framed glasses she wore for driving, gave her the look of a strict but sexy schoolteacher.

'Oh, you! My wedding ring won't come off anyway, so that might just give the game away.'

'Ok, me it is. We'll say it's a second marriage, and we're planning for around eighty guests. Does that sound about right?'

'Yes, perfect. We'll say it's for next summer, too; I expect they're fully booked for months. Don't take the next exit, take the one after. It's a faster road.'

'OK.'

They drove on in silence for a few miles. Claire signalled to turn left, then glanced over at Jenny.

'I get the feeling your Paul doesn't like me very much! He wasn't very welcoming when I turned up on the doorstep. But I can't blame him; he's protective and he thinks I'm leading you into danger.'

'Not danger exactly – he doesn't take it that seriously. He thinks it's a wild goose chase, and that you're wasting my time,' said Jenny. She was still fuming at Paul's behaviour. 'He doesn't like to have his routine changed. He likes to be in charge. Me going off for the day has put him in a foul mood.'

They had had a bad argument the week before, when Jenny had asked if he could pick up the boys from school one day the following week.

'That might be difficult. It's a crazy week. Lots of meetings. Why? What's so important?' he'd said.

Jenny had taken a deep breath. 'Well,' she started, 'Claire and I are driving over to Yorkshire. We're going to take a look at the old house we used to play in. It's a posh hotel now, apparently.'

'Oh, for God's sake, not that again! What *is* the point?'

'Well, it might stir some memories. And if not, it'll be a nice day out and a chance for me and Claire to have a good chat. I owe her that much at least.'

'What about what you owe me? The kids? You've been so distracted this week. You've barely spoken to us. You've been messing about doing internet searches every evening.'

Jenny was speechless with indignation for a moment. Then she argued back:

'Hah, you hypocrite! Says the man who never gets home before eight pm! When have you spent much time with the boys lately? It's me who does everything in the house, and with the boys!'

'But I am building something for our future. I'm working my bollocks off. You don't realise how hard it is. I would love to come home at five every evening, but I can't.' His voice had been getting more and more heated and his blue eyes had been flashing with real anger. Now he took a deep breath and made an effort to appear calm and conciliatory. 'Look, I'd love for you to go off to a nice hotel, have a coffee and a long chat with your oldest friend. But not right now. It's not possible.'

Jenny would normally have backed down at this point, but something made her grit her teeth and push through.

'I *am* going to Yorkshire with Claire next week. You pick

the day that suits you. You might have to reschedule a meeting, but that's just the way it is. This is important to me.'

They had barely spoken since. That morning, Paul had opened the door to Claire with a stony face, then fetched his car keys and left the house without a word.

'He's being a real dick, to be honest,' she said now to Claire. 'I've never known him like this before. I thought we had an equal partnership, but I'm beginning to wonder.'

'Do you still love him?'

Jenny was taken aback by the blunt question. Did she love him? Had that changed? She thought back over the many years they had spent together. They'd met in their second year at university. Paul had come crashing into the communal kitchen of her student residence late one evening. She'd recognised him at once: he was one of the golden boys, popular and assured. She often saw him in the union building, surrounded by friends, holding court.

'Is Sarah here?' he'd asked, looking around impatiently.

'Sarah? No, I haven't seen her today. Have you checked her room? It's number five.'

'Yes, I knocked, but there's no answer,' he'd said. Then he'd looked at her properly for the first time and continued: 'I'm supposed to be taking her to a party. Oh well. Her loss. Do you want to come instead?'

Why the hell not? she'd thought, and surprised herself by accepting. The party had been a dead loss, but they had talked all night.

'What course are you on?' Her first question was not exactly original.

'Computing.'

'No way! I thought all computer nerds were supposed to have glasses and spots and mild Asperger's, and wear socks with sandals. You look more like you should be doing Politics and

Economics and being chair of the Conservative party!'

'You had me down as a Tory? God forbid! I *am* chair of the Ethical Hacking Society though.'

'Ethical hacking? Sounds like an oxymoron to me! What do you get up to in that, then?'

'Ah, well, if I told you that, I'd have to kill you. So what course are you on?'

'Geography with languages. Specialising in urban geography.'

'Really? I've always wondered what people do with a geography degree. Sounds completely fucking useless to me!'

'Cheeky bugger! No it's brilliant. I want to work in town planning eventually. What about you?'

'Oh, I'll be running my own business in a year or two and making a fortune.'

Jenny found his confidence refreshing. It made a change from the normal student angst. She was intrigued by this man, so far removed from her usual type.

'Whereabouts are you from?' she asked.

'Dundee.'

'Now I *really* don't believe you. Where's your Scottish accent?'

'I went to an English boarding school. A bit like Tony Blair. No, actually he went to Fettes College in Edinburgh. But anyway, I am Scottish.'

'Pseudo-Scottish. What a waste. There's nothing sexier than a Scottish accent.'

'So you're saying I'm not sexy?'

'You've definitely dropped down a couple of points. Sorry about that.'

'Go on then, where are you from?'

'Wakefield, in Yorkshire.'

'Ha! Now who's the pseudo? You don't have a Yorkshire accent!'

'I do a bit. I say 'bath' and 'glass' not 'barth' and 'glarse'. Flat vowels.'

'Totally fake. Go on, say this word.' He dipped his finger into his beer glass and wrote the word 'bus' on his forearm.

'Bus!' she said, trying to sound as Yorkshire as she could.

'That was rubbish! I bet your dad doesn't even work down t' pit!'

'Ooh, that is such horrendous stereotyping! Like me saying I bet your dad wears nothing under his kilt.'

'He doesn't actually. Totally bollock naked under there.'

They had talked nonsense until they were thrown out of the party in the small hours, and then ended up back in her student room, first sharing a bottle of vodka and then sharing kisses. At the end of term, he'd invited her to meet his parents in their beautiful stone cottage in the Angus countryside. Jenny immediately warmed to his dad, but had been terrified of his formidable French mother. Paul had, in turn, visited her parents in Yorkshire, effortlessly charming them both. A bit too effortlessly, if she was honest; he had laid on the charm a little too thick at times. Her mother had been in raptures.

She had been attracted to this man from the start; his exotic half-Scottish-half-French heritage, his incredible energy and self-belief, which made her, in turn, feel that she could achieve almost anything. She was amazed that this golden man had chosen her. Those early student years had been full of fun and excitement; they would drink and party and make love for hours.

They married relatively young. Jenny got her dream job in town planning, and Paul had started with a less than perfect job as an IT support worker. Not long after, they discovered that

Jenny was pregnant, and shared the exhilaration and the strain of becoming parents. She remembered his awed expression as he held a new-born Jake in his arms. He'd been very much a hands-on father, helping with nappies and feeding. Then came Davie. Those early years had been tough, exhausting even, but they had struggled through together. She thought back to all those family holidays they'd enjoyed, playing cricket on the beach, building complex sandcastles, eating sandy picnics. Paul had spent many hours patiently teaching the boys to swim, or how to do a rugby drop kick. He had been such a great dad when they were little. And a tender, caring husband. They laughed often. The sex had been frequent and good. Right now, she couldn't remember the last time they'd made love. What did that mean? Was it partly her fault for being so irritated with him? She recognised the signs of his interest – the hand on her thigh, or the decisive way he closed his book and put it on the bedside table, but more often than not, she chose to ignore them. Yes, she had her share of the blame. It wasn't all his fault. He was still the same man. He was just under a lot of pressure right now.

Jenny snapped back to the present. 'Yes, yes I do still love him!' she said to Claire now. 'I just need to reset the balance a bit! He's got too used to me falling in with him all the time. Anyway, changing the subject, what did you think of that article I sent you last night?'

'Oh, it's definitely interesting! This Tommy Whitaker character started off as a bit of a gangster, reading between the lines. He ran nightclubs and massage parlours in Leeds, back in the 90s. That's often shorthand for prostitution. And now he's reinventing himself as a pillar of the community.'

'Is he connected to your flashbacks?'

Claire gave an enigmatic smile. 'I'm not saying anything just now. But I've got something to show you later, when we've seen the house.'

A few minutes later, they rounded a corner and Jenny saw magnificent stone gateposts topped with rampant lions. The shiny metal gates stood wide open, and a tasteful aubergine-coloured board with gold lettering announced:

Blackmere Hall

Hotel and Country Club

*****

'Wow, five stars! God, it can't be the same place surely?'

They drove through the gates and along the sweeping gravel driveway that cut through the mature trees. The main car park was located in a cleared area of woodland, each parking space delineated by narrow wooden logs. They got out of the car and walked up to the rustic wooden signpost indicating 'The Hall' in one direction, and 'Nature Trail' in the other.

'Which first?' asked Jenny.

'The house, I think. Let's go.'

And seconds later, there it was, rather magnificent in the mid-morning sunshine. The formal gardens were neat, the hedges clipped and the lawns cut short and meticulously striped. The statues had gone, but in their place, two imposing stone urns held pyramids of shaped box, while further up the path, the fountain gently released water into the three tiered basins. The old perimeter walls had not been restored, but were still blackened and crumbling, the contrast with the formal garden giving the whole a wildly romantic appeal.

And there was the house, beautifully symmetrical, the stonework pale gold and the windows sparkling. No ivy marred the façade, and no moss had gathered on the wide stone steps leading to the huge oak door.

'Ready to play the future bride?' asked Jenny.

'Oh yeah!' grinned Claire, and they pushed open the door and walked inside.

The entrance hall was much more hotel-like. The black and white tiled floor was polished to a high shine, and comfortable armchairs stood in clusters around elegant side tables. The broad staircase to the right was carpeted in deep red plush. To the left was a reception area, and beyond that, an open doorway gave a glimpse of a wood-panelled bar.

The young receptionist smiled brightly up at them as they approached.

'Good morning. Can I help you?'

'Yes, I hope so. I'm actually getting married next year and I'm looking for a place to hold the reception. Is it OK if we have a look around?'

'Well, yes of course! This is a wonderful place for a wedding reception. Let me put a call through to our wedding planner, and see if she's free just now. She can give you the grand tour.'

A full hour later, Claire's patience was beginning to fray. They had identified the best function room for the number of guests, the number of bedrooms required for guests staying over, the type of evening function preferred. They had talked about menus and even visited the bridal suite.

'God, I'm even starting to believe it myself!' she complained to Jenny, as the wedding planner went off to fetch some price lists. 'Remind me never to get married again! What a marathon!'

The woman hurried towards them with a folder, her heels clicking on the polished floor. 'Here you are. Now, would you both like a complementary drink at the bar while you look through the price lists?' she asked.

But Claire had had enough of weddings. 'Oh, yes, maybe in a moment or two,' she said, smiling politely. 'That would be great. But just another question first. What about photos? Where do people have their photos taken? Is it in front of the house? Or down by the lake?'

'Oh, there are hundreds of great places for photos. Group shots on the lawn, intimate couple shots in the woods. And most couples like to have their photo taken looking out over the lake. It's very romantic.'

'Ooh, that sounds lovely. Can we go and have a look at that now?'

'Yes of course. Take your time. Just let me know when you want that drink. It's on the house.'

They walked quickly out of the building, relieved to be free of the gushing saleswoman. Jenny was light-headed, laughing, full of admiration for Claire's inventive skills.

'You were brilliant!' she said, expecting Claire to join in her laughter. 'I want to be chief bridesmaid! When can we start looking at dresses? And just a warning - I'm vetoing pink.'

But Claire's blue eyes were serious. She looked pale and exhausted all of a sudden.

'Are you OK? 'asked Jenny. 'I'm sorry, I'm such an idiot. It must have been hard to talk about weddings and stuff when you've only fairly recently divorced. It must bring it all back.'

'No, it's not that. That was all quite fun really. But that's not why we're here. Let's walk down to the trees, then back towards the lake, and see if it jogs your memory.'

Jenny felt a stab of guilt. She had been enjoying the role-play, treating it as a rather frivolous adventure, but for Claire this exercise was about proving that her sanity was intact. Chastened, she followed Claire across the lawns, down the path and into the first line of trees. They stopped for a moment under a broad chestnut tree, then looked back towards the house. Jenny tried hard to search her memory. Nothing. The house looked smart, inviting, and very business-like. Then she looked to the left. The lake sparkled in the late morning sunshine. Two swans glided serenely across the surface and on the far shore, rhododendrons and weeping willows were reflected beautifully in the still waters. She was about to turn away when something caught her eye.

'Is that the jetty? It's... There's something about that jetty, isn't there?'

Claire let out a long sigh of relief. 'Oh my God! Yes! Yes! Oh, thank God! You're starting to remember. I'm not going mad! There is indeed something about the jetty.'

Jenny concentrated hard. She felt she was on the point of visualising something, a flash of movement, a colour... It was almost within reach, but then it slipped away, lost.

'I had a flash of something but it's gone again. Will you tell me now?'

'OK. Let's get out of here. We'll go and get a pub lunch somewhere and I'll tell you everything.'

9

Summer 1990

Jenny shook out the picnic blanket and set it down under the chestnut tree. Then she and Claire carefully laid out their stakeout kit: two packs of Jaffa cakes, a bottle of lemonade, binoculars, notebook and pens, spare cardigans. They were prepared for the long haul. They had dressed carefully that morning in camouflage colours; green jumpers and black trousers. Jenny had also suggested they black out their faces with mud. From their position, hidden from view under the low-spreading branches, they had a good view of the house, the gardens and the lake. This was going to be fun!

'Isn't this brilliant! It's a real adventure,' said Jenny. 'Have you read *Five Get into a Fix?* They break into the grounds of the old house with the tower on the hill, with the Keep Out sign. They see a face at the window. And they solve the mystery. I can't remember what the mystery was now. In fact I think the story was a bit stupid, actually. But this is so cool!'

An hour later, they were cold and bored. They had noted down the registration of the blue car, parked outside the house. But there had been absolutely no movement from inside the house. The Jaffa cakes were finished and their legs were stiff.

'Let's go home,' said Jenny. 'This is boring now.'

'Just a bit longer. It's our last chance today. The Caretaker's bound to come out sometime. I'm sure that must be his car.'

Half an hour passed. Jenny yawned and started fiddling with a Jaffa cakes packet, tearing the cardboard into little pieces. She glanced over at Claire, wondering if it was too soon to suggest going home again. Then they heard a noise. The sound of tyres scrunching over gravel. Suddenly alert, they saw a big black car pull up to the house, the white TAXI CAB sign unlit.

'Quick, get the binoculars! Can you see the number plate?'

The driver got out and opened the rear door.

'Someone's getting out of the back!'

'Can you see who it is?'

'No, the car's in the way.'

But then the taxi turned in a wide arc to make its way back down the drive and they could see clearly who it was. A lady. Long legs clad in knee-high boots. A short red skirt or dress, which could just be glimpsed underneath an oversize denim jacket. The woman had beautiful long auburn hair, almost reaching her waist, which she tossed as she walked up the steps and into the house.

'Gosh, she's beautiful!' breathed Claire. 'She looks like a film star!'

'Or a model. She look like Cindy Crawford!'

'What's she doing with the Caretaker? He's so ugly!'

'Maybe they're in league. They found the treasure and they're going to divide it up.'

Again they waited, scanning the house with the binoculars from time to time. Once Claire thought she caught a glimpse of movement from one of the upstairs windows. Another hour passed and Jenny looked nervously at her Mickey Mouse watch.

'It's getting near tea time now. I think we should pack up and go home.'

'Oh, OK,' Claire agreed, reluctantly. But just then there was movement. The big oak door was flung wide open. Then nothing.

'What's happening?'

'I don't know! But we've got to wait now.'

And then he appeared in the doorway. The Caretaker. He was carrying what looked like a rolled up carpet. It seemed heavy, and he hefted it more securely in his arms as he made his way carefully down the stone steps. The carpet sagged strangely between his arms, forming a zig-zag shape.

'What do you think that is? Maybe it's a priceless oriental carpet and he's stealing it!'

'Or he's stealing priceless weapons – you know, like old swords and spears and stuff that were hanging on the walls.'

But instead of crossing to where the blue car waited, the man continued through the weeds and high grasses and down towards the lake. When he reached the jetty, he put the carpet down on the wooden boards, stood up and stretched, holding onto his lower back. Then he crouched down over the carpet.

'What's he doing?' asked Claire. 'Let me have a go with the binoculars.'

'I can't see. Here, you have a go.'

'He's lifting up the carpet and putting it in the rowing boat.'

'That's weird.'

'Now he's picking up the oars. He's rowing out into the lake.'

'Yeah, I can see that.'

Claire put the binoculars down and they both watched as the Caretaker pulled out into the lake with strong stokes. Then he stopped and replaced the oars inside. The boat started to drift slightly towards their hiding place in the woods, giving the girls a clear view. He stood up, making the little boat rock alarmingly, and forcing him to replant his feet and throw out his arms for balance. When the rocking subsided, he bent down, lifting up the carpet, which now seemed to have something tied around it. A sudden gust of wind made the boat turn and the man almost lost his balance. He took a step to the side and the object in his arms slipped suddenly downwards in his grasp. He quickly regained control, but not before the girls clearly saw what was in his arms. The afternoon sunshine caught the twist of auburn hair which had tumbled free from the end of the roll and cascaded down, almost touching the water.

They stared, mesmerized, as the stiffening breeze played with the glossy strands. The moment seemed frozen in time. Gawping, open mouthed, they scarcely dared to breathe.

Then there was a splash, and the spell was broken. The man looked down into the depths as the body sank lower and lower. He rubbed his hands together with satisfaction, wiped them on his denim-covered thighs and sat back down to take up the oars.

'Get down!' hissed Jenny, as the boat started to turn. They threw themselves onto the ground, eyes tight shut, not daring to watch, but listening instead to the faint rippling noise as the oars pushed against the water. They heard a scrape as the rowing boat bumped against the jetty. They waited, heartbeats hammering, for several more minutes, before finding the courage to look up.

All was quiet. It was as if nothing had happened. The lake sparkled prettily. A trio of geese glided gracefully above the surface, then flapped their wings just once as they lifted their feet to land. The boat was once again tied up innocently alongside the jetty. At the house, the big oak door was shut.

Jenny and Claire locked eyes without speaking. Minutes passed before one of them could find their voice.

'Did you s-?' started Claire.

But Jenny interrupted. 'No. No.' She shook her head, as if trying to clear the vision from her memory. 'Come on. It's really late. We've got to go home.'

'But...'

'Come on. That was... No. I don't want to talk about it... Let's put everything away and go home. I'm starving.'

Claire gave her a bewildered look, but followed Jenny's lead, picking up the notebook and binoculars and handing them to her friend. They walked quickly back to their bikes, cycled home, ate chocolate cake at tea-time and, as a special treat for their last night together, fish and chips for supper. Neither wanted to talk. Instead they watched some TV with the family and went to bed late.

The next morning, Claire's parents came to collect her. The girls stayed in the living room and watched as the grown-ups chatted over coffee. They hugged tightly as Ken put the case into the boot of his old white Renault.

'Write soon!' begged Jenny.

'I will!' said Claire.

Jenny watched the car until it disappeared round the corner and then went back into her house. Normally miserable each time they parted, she was surprised to feel something akin to relief.

It was she who wrote the first letter. It contained the detailed description of a whole, new pretend family, peopled with characters that she had total control of. There was three-year old Amy, who was naughty but cute, six year-old Mark who was brave and adventurous and sixteen year-old Stephanie, moody, spiteful and superior. These were people who did predictable things in a safe and cosy world. Rosie would steal the chocolate buttons from the cake her mother had just made. Mark would climb a tree and get stuck. Stephanie would accidentally dye her hair purple. Jenny wrapped her pretend family around her like a comfort blanket, secure in the knowledge that she could keep them all safe.

If Claire had wanted to write back about what they had seen that afternoon by the lake, she never did. Jenny's letter sent a clear message: the subject was closed. It was not referred to on their next holiday together.

Maybe it had never happened.

10

The weather changed suddenly, as it often does in Yorkshire. As they left the towns behind and drove out towards the moors, the landscape became more bleak and rugged. Claire looked in the rear-view mirror and saw black clouds gathering. How appropriate for the conversation we're about to have, she thought. The road twisted and climbed to the highest point of Holme Moss, with its jaw-dropping views over the West Yorkshire countryside below, then continued down into greener, gentler valleys as they approached Cheshire. Pretty stone villages began to appear. She saw a traditional stone pub on the crest of the hill and pulled into the car park. The Black Bull was warm and welcoming. A fire was lit in the huge stone fireplace. Blackboards over the bar displayed a tempting selection of home-cooked bar meals. They ordered food and halves of beer at the bar, carried their drinks to a corner table, and took a long gulp, before looking at each other.

'So...'

'So...'

'How much do you remember now?' asked Claire.

'I remember hiding in the trees. I remember being really scared. And I remember something happened at the jetty. But that's about it.'

'Nothing more about the jetty?'

'Um, some movement, noise, a kind of blur. Nothing else.'

Claire nodded slowly. 'OK. I'll tell you everything I remember.'

As she started to talk, Jenny nodded occasionally. There was a pause when the barmaid brought their meals to the table, but as soon as she'd left, Claire continued between mouthfuls of steak pie. When she finished speaking, she stood up and said:

'I'm off to the loo. Then I'll get us a couple of coffees, shall I? Give you time to take it all in.'

Jenny stayed in her seat, trying to piece Claire's story together with her own memories. She could visualise it now; the man on the jetty, the roll of carpet, the splash. It seemed so clear, so vivid, but was that because Claire had given such a good description, or was her own memory kicking in at last? She had no idea. When Claire came back with the coffees she tried to put everything together:

'So, we saw this man dump the body of a woman in the lake.'

'Yes.'

'And this man was the one we called the Caretaker?'

'Yes.'

'But we don't know who he is.'

'Well... maybe we do. Did you bring that arts committee magazine with you?'

'Yes, here.' Jenny pulled it out of her rapacious handbag and opened it out to the centre pages.

'Look at this,' said Claire, fishing something out of her own bag. It was a school exercise book, covered in orange wallpaper. Jenny felt an instant flash of recognition.

'Oh my God! The Mystery Book! You kept it!'

'I did. Here, have a look.' She handed the book over to Jenny, who opened it almost reverently. The Sellotape holding the cover together was crispy, brown and lifting away. The first

page showed the title: *The Mystery Book. Dead Secret. Hands off.*
The next pages explained their theory in loopy handwriting
and very poor spelling:

*We think the people in the house murdered there children and
berried them in the woods because they didn't want children.*

*We think they stole some money and berried it in the secret
house in the woods. Then they died and the house was empty for
hundreds of years.*

There followed a map of the grounds in green and red felt
tip, with each grave marked and the ice-house crudely drawn.
Jenny traced the map with her finger. It was so familiar to her.
She could remember drawing it at the kitchen table. They'd
done the trees together, Claire making pretty round ones, and
herself making tall, spiky firs. She turned the page. Pictures of
each 'gravestone', with the lettering and dates they had noted
down.

*We think the Caretaker found the tresure and took it to the
house. We think he wants to steel the tresure for himself.*

Next, a tracing of a large, old-fashioned key, coloured in
with brown felt tip.

*We found the key and went in the house. It was really spooky.
Now the Caretaker has seen us! He knows who we are and can be
dangerus.*

*We have to find out what the Caretaker is up to. We are going to
do a stay cowt.*

Jenny smiled as she turned each page, releasing a flood
of poignant memories. But on the last page was a picture that
made her gasp. A clumsily drawn figure, with exaggerated arms.
A square face, framed by red, curly hair. A large nose. And a scar,
which ran from eyebrow to cheek, half-closing one eye.

Jenny took the magazine and laid the two images side by
side. The hair. The scar. Was it a coincidence?

'You think Tommy Whitaker is the murderer?'

'I'm sure of it. Absolutely. I can remember the man with the scar throwing a body into the lake. It was the body of a woman. I saw the long brown hair. And it's got to be the same man as in the art magazine.'

Jenny nodded slowly. 'But what can we do about it? It's so long ago. I mean, no-one would ever believe us after all this time.'

'I'm not sure what to do. At first I just wanted to know... to know if these memories were real or not. Now I think we've proved that. But I don't think I can let it go there. I think we've got to do something.'

'Well, we can't just go to the police and say we saw a murder happen when we were ten years old. We'd be laughed out of the police station.'

'I know. We need a bit more information. So I want to do more research. Find out about Tommy Whitaker's past. And then go to the police.'

'Why is it so important to you? Don't you think it would be safer just to let it drop? This might be really dangerous.'

Claire sighed, sat back in her chair and gave Jenny a direct look.

'I'm, um...' she started. 'I'm struggling a bit with life at the moment. I've lost my confidence. I can't see the way forward. There are things I can't let myself think about. Things that are too painful. Mike is going to be a father in a few weeks. It just fills me with rage. It's not fair. I can't help it. If I think too long about that I'll just go into a spiral again. I've got to block that out. And I can do that by keeping busy, having projects. This is my project. Solving the mystery. Finding out who was killed and why. If I can do that, well, my life has some direction at least.'

'But it's all a kind of displacement, isn't it?' asked Jenny, gently. 'Avoidance. At some stage you have to sit down and face up to things that are really painful. Then you can start to get over them.'

'I can't take the risk. Not yet. If I open that box I might fall down the hole again.'

'Fall down the hole... You said you 'did something stupid' before. Did you mean...?'

Claire paused, fiddling with her coffee spoon and weighing up how much to say and how much to hide. Eventually she glanced up and said:

'I took pills. Tried to kill myself.'

'Oh, Claire! Oh no! I'm so sorry. I don't know what to say. When I look at you I see someone who's very brave, very beautiful, who's vivacious and fun...'

'Hah, maybe in the past. I'm not so much fun these days,' Claire interrupted with a sad smile.

'But you were great fun and you will be again. Listen.' She grabbed Claire's hand to emphasize her words. 'You're... you were always my role model when we were young. I copied everything you did - your clothes, your books, your haircuts – I even tried to copy your handwriting. You're still my role model! You look great! I love what you're wearing today, for example. Just look at you! You're so stylish.' She pointed to Claire's classic grey lambswool pullover, which somehow brought out the colour of her very blue eyes and set off her white-blonde hair. But she also noted the tendons which were visible in Claire's throat and the way her collarbone stood out so sharply. She really was much too thin. 'You even look good in your glasses! Mine make me look like a hundred year-old librarian, but yours are so cool. I don't think you have any idea how beautiful you are. But it's not just how you look. I just mean that, for me, you're bloody perfect. And don't let what that arsehole of a husband did make you forget that!'

'Thanks. You're kind,' said Claire, smiling, but her voice had little conviction.

'It will get better. It will! What does your therapist say?'

'Oh he's a bit useless. He just talks about being kind to yourself, not expecting too much of yourself. He thinks I should take up a hobby, grow tomatoes, join a theatre group, learn to play the piano… He's not much good as a therapist, to be honest. But he's free with the NHS. I can't afford a proper one!'

'Well, he sounds OK to me. It's all good advice, I suppose. We all need to be kinder to ourselves. Did you tell him about the body in the lake?'

'No. Not yet. I'm saving that little nugget. He will absolutely… cream himself when he hears that. I suspect it's all his theories come true. Childhood trauma. Trust issues. Fear of men. Being too passive in my marriage. He's going to enjoy that far too much.'

'So you don't think what we saw that day was the reason you've had problems?'

'No. I don't.'

'I hope not. I feel bad because, from what you say, it was me who kind of shut it down when we were kids. Refused to talk about it. Maybe if we'd spoken to each other a lot more at the time… Or if we'd actually told someone, told my parents…'

'We were too young. We coped the best way we knew how. Anyway, you went on to have a very normal life, a happy marriage, no big mental issues.'

'Huh, not so sure about the happy marriage bit just now…' Jenny grimaced, then shrugged. 'But yeah, my life's OK I guess. No, it's good. Mostly. So, what now? What do we do?'

'I'm going to follow the money. I didn't train as an accountant for nothing. I want to know how he made enough money to get his hotel chain. Was there illegal activity. Did he cheat on his tax. That kind of thing.'

'What can I do?'

'Just keep trying to remember stuff.'

'OK. Will do.' She twisted in her seat to look out of the pub window. 'Now, shall we make the most of the day and go for a walk or something? It looks like it's stopped raining and I don't want to go home just yet. What are your shoes like?'

'Not too bad. They've got a bit of grip. Yes, let's go.'

They found a sign for a footpath a little further on, parked up and followed the dry stone wall up to the top of the moor, avoiding the mud as best they could. Then they struck out along the ridge, taking in the views of bare hillsides criss-crossed by walls, studded with stone farmhouses and dotted with sheep. By unspoken consent, they stuck to lighter subjects.

'Do you remember the time John fell in the river? We were staying at the farm in Swaledale. He was teasing us, pretending to fall in, and then the bank really did give way, and he fell in, right up to his neck. We had to pull him out.'

'Yes! I remember. He was so mad. And do you remember when we tried to get into that film? It must have been rated 15 or something. We borrowed your mum's make up – blue eye shadow and coral-red lipstick, and we must have looked younger than ever. We didn't stand a chance.'

'Some of my favourite memories are going to the beach from your house. We used to walk through the pine forests and there was the beach, all sparkling – I lived so far from the sea that the beach seemed like a tropical paradise to me. I was so jealous.'

'Oh, I used to love coming to yours! Your dad would take us all over the place in the car. We had pub lunches and picnics and he'd tell us about castles and battles. I was jealous of your dad! I mean, my dad's great, but yours...'

'It was your mum I really loved. She was always up for anything, like a super-friendly gym mistress. All jolly hockey sticks and raring to go. My mum used to sit in the car and do knitting while me and Dad and John walked up the mountains.'

As they reminisced, Jenny felt the bond between them knitting ever closer. They laughed as they slipped in the mud and helped each other over awkward styles. The fifteen missing years melted away as if by magic. This is brilliant, I've got my best friend back, she thought. I want to help her get strong again. If only the Blackmere Hall stuff would just go away. It's confusing and unsettling, and I don't know how to deal with it.

***

Jenny waved as Claire reversed her car back down the drive. She hadn't invited her in. She opened the door to the sound of Jake and Davie squabbling in the living room. She threw her bag and coat over the bannister and went to see what the problem was.

'Hi boys, I'm back. What are you two fighting about?'

'*Muuuum*,' wailed Davie, his little face screwed up with indignation. 'Jake broke my Lego spaceship. I only just finished it.' Jake was sitting some way off with his arms crossed, his lower lip sticking out sulkily.

'I'm sure he didn't do it on purpose.' Jenny was actually not sure at all. 'Jake, you can help your brother fix it. Come here and help find all the pieces. Where's your Dad?'

'Upstairs in the study, I think.'

Jenny sighed and went into the kitchen. As she opened the fridge to see what she could make for dinner, she heard Paul's feet on the stairs.

'You're back,' he said. 'How was your little day trip? Did you solve the great murder mystery, then?'

'Well, yes, we did in a way. Something did happen. We saw a man throw a body into a lake.'

'Really? Are you sure you actually saw that?'

'Well...yes, almost sure.'

'Almost. Right. And you didn't tell anyone?'

'No.'

'And then you forgot all about it?'

'Yes.'

'Pfft.' Paul gave an almost imperceptible sarcastic snort. 'N'importe quoi,' he muttered under his breath, annoyingly.

'What? What did you say?' She hated it when he spoke in French.

'Nothing, nothing.' Paul smiled, a little condescendingly. 'Look, I'm really glad you solved the mystery. That's great. Your friend will be happy. Now, why don't we get a take-away? I'll fetch the menus. Curry or kebabs?'

Jenny watched his retreating back as he went to find the menus. He was whistling jauntily, hands in his pockets. That's it, she thought. He thinks it's all over now. End of story. Back to normal. She was irritated by Paul's dismissal, but she also knew, in her heart of hearts, she didn't want to take things any further. She'd done what Claire had asked, and now it was time to leave well alone. Let sleeping bodies lie. Yes, maybe it really was all over now.

But it turned out to be only the beginning.

11

'Hi! It's me. Is this a good time? I think I've got the dirt on Tommy Whitaker now.'

Jenny's heart sank. She closed her eyes briefly and gripped the receiver a bit more tightly in her left hand.

She had been miles away, absorbed in the process of creating her art. Her right hand held a fine sable paintbrush, dipped in thinned-down acrylic and poised to place the narrow slash of black pupil in the centre of the cat's green eye. The portrait was going well. She had limited time to finish it and her first guilty reaction was to resent this unwelcome interruption.

She had put the visit to Blackmere Hall firmly out of her mind for several days. She told herself that if you chase a memory, it only becomes more and more elusive. Carrying on as normal would be the best way – and the memories would filter back in their own good time. She'd established a workable truce with Paul. Claire wasn't mentioned and they were each being extra attentive to the other. Paul was still working late most nights, but at the weekend he'd suggested a family trip to the zoo. Davie had been ecstatic, but Jake had been typically snooty at the idea, complaining that zoos were too babyish for a ten-year old. However, even he had been entranced by the baby black rhino, cavorting gaily around its mother on stubby little legs. Paul and Jenny had held hands as the four of them leaned over the wooden barriers to watch the cheetahs in the enclosure below, and Jenny had felt an unaccustomed stab of complete happiness. This was what was important; her marriage, her boys, the family.

Now, Jenny placed her paintbrush back into the jam jar of water with a sigh.

'Hang on a minute,' she said. 'I've just got to wipe my hands. OK. Fire away.'

'Right,' Claire sounded excited. 'What do you know about money laundering?'

'Absolutely nothing!'

'OK. I've done a lot of digging into financial records and tax statements and stuff. So, basically, I'm pretty sure that Tommy Whitaker was into all kinds of illegal activities in the late eighties and nineties. Officially, he owned two nightclubs, a strip club, four pizza restaurants, a nail bar, a massage parlour and a tanning parlour.'

'Wow! So many places? He would have been quite young at the time though, don't you think? Late twenties, early thirties? How did he get all that so fast?'

'That's not clear. Maybe he forced the previous owners to sell, I don't know. Now, those businesses all made extraordinary amounts of money. I mean, crazy sums, unlikely sums. And they weren't located in the posh parts of Leeds. We're talking about Beeston, Chapeltown, Belle Isle, Cross Green... So where do you think the money came from?'

'Drugs?'

'Yep, that's my guess. Plus prostitution, illegal gambling, that kind of thing. So, when you get huge amounts of cash coming in, you massively inflate your takings in your legal activities. Then you bank the cash in some deposit-taking financial establishment and start moving it around between different accounts in different names. It's called 'layering'. You create a complex trail that's almost impossible to follow. Tommy Whitaker had several accounts in different names, I think.

Money was moved to an account in Switzerland for a Tomas Terre'Blanche for example - that could be him, don't you think? Terre'Blanche, White Land, Whitaker?'

'How on earth did you find all this out?'

'Well, I've called in lots of favours with former colleagues and contacts in banks and at the tax office. I haven't got any firm proof, but there's a hell of a lot of leads that need following up. Anyhow, once you've disguised your cash and hidden it amongst various accounts, you then spend it on high value items like yachts, gold – or property. Hey presto, your money is clean. Legit. And that's what Tommy Whitaker did. He bought Blackmere Hall in 1990, then followed with a string of crumbling old country houses in the next ten years that he converted into country-club hotels. It is notoriously difficult to make a profit from this type of hotel. They are really expensive to restore, and to operate. My guess is that he's still using these hotels to launder drug money. What do you think?'

'Wow... well...wow! I don't know. You say you don't have any proof, though. It's not enough to go to the police with, is it?'

'I think it is. Especially if we connect it to what we saw. And there's more. Listen to this!'

Jenny's head was spinning, but she forced herself to concentrate, as Claire continued:

'There's a website called Leeds Missing Persons. It's for relatives to write a description of the person they've lost, ask for any information or beg that person to get in touch. There are pages and pages of entries. I've spent all week collating them and sorting them – looking for disappearances in the nineties, young women, brown hair, et cetera. Anyway, the upshot is, thirty-eight young women went missing in Leeds in the early nineties. And seven of them could have had a connection to Tommy Whitaker!'

'Bloody hell! What do you mean? What kind of connection?'

'They all worked in nightclubs or strip joints and lived in those parts of the city.'

'But you don't know for sure that they worked in Tommy Whitaker's clubs?'

'No,' Claire admitted. 'No, I don't. But what are the chances?'

'Are you saying you think he's a multiple murderer?'

'Not necessarily. But he could be!'

'Did this missing persons site show photos of the girls?'

'Yes, most of the posts included a photo; several of very pretty women with long brown hair.'

'Good God. This is... I don't like this.' Jenny found that she was shivering. What was the expression, she wondered, a goose walking over her grave? Silly expression. Why a goose? She pushed the thought of graves away. 'Claire, this is all getting too dark for me. Can we just drop it? Please? I'm scared!'

'I'm scared too. But think of all the families that are still hoping for news of their loved ones, thirty years later. And think of that bastard running for election onto the city council. We can't let him get away with it.'

'Can't we just send what we've got anonymously to a newspaper? Let them do the digging?'

'No, I'm worried it might just end up in someone's in-tray and nothing would ever get done. I want to go to the police. So... Jenny, will you come with me?'

Jenny took a long moment to think. As much as she hated this, she knew that Paul was going to hate it even more. This might shatter the delicate alliance they'd recreated over the last two weeks. But on the other hand, this was her oldest friend, and she needed support.

'What will you do if I say no?'

'I'll go on my own.'

'Oh, God,' she sighed. 'All right then. You win. I'll come with you.'

'Thank you, thank you! You are amazing! Let's go one day next week.'

When Jenny finally replaced the handset in its holder, she sat with her elbows on the table, her chin supported in her two hands and her eyes closed. Her thoughts raced. Her main concern was - what the hell am I going to say to Paul?

But that should have been the last thing to worry about. Things were about to be set in motion, and her cosy suburban lifestyle was about to be stripped away, leaving her shivering, exposed – and terrified.

12

The police station was not at all what they had expected from watching various crime series on TV. Jenny had imagined a run-down façade, an interior of institutional green walls, and a bored-looking officer leaning nonchalantly on the counter of the reception desk. Instead, this was an imposing modern building of gleaming glass and steel. It could have been the headquarters of a successful bank or insurance company. They had phoned ahead, and now sat nervously in the pristine waiting area, watching the people come and go with bewildering efficiency.

It all seemed unreal to Jenny, as if they'd been roped into a police drama as extras. She tried to order her thoughts, to imagine what they were going to say, but every sentence sounded ridiculous in her ears. 'We saw a murder when we were ten.' Pathetic. How on earth was that going to carry any weight, when these busy, professional people were dealing with a daily stream of burglaries, domestic abuse, drunken fights? This is a mistake. We shouldn't have come.

Claire sat staring straight ahead, clutching her briefcase protectively on her lap. She had dressed conservatively in a smart black trouser suit, but Jenny could see that her foot was jiggling up and down incessantly on the polished concrete floor. She was nervous too.

After a long wait, they saw a harried looking woman in uniform conferring with the reception staff, then looking over towards them. She was in her late fifties, with a short, almost manly haircut. There was no smile as she walked towards them in brisk strides, and Jenny's apprehension deepened.

'Ms Hastings? Ms Kerr? My name is Detective Inspector Fielding. If you'd like to follow me?'

She lead the way up the stairs and along a featureless corridor, before stopping at a door and inviting them to enter. The room was equally bland; white walls, a Formica desk with tidily stacked papers and four hard blue chairs. On another desk stood recording equipment and what looked like a fax machine. As the two women sat down, Jenny felt her face going red. She couldn't help feeling that she was the criminal, guilty of something for sure, if maybe only wasting police time. She glanced across at Claire, who seemed calm but very pale.

'Now, I understand you want to report a crime?'

Claire took the lead: 'Yes, that's right. It's an old crime. It happened in 1990. We saw a man dispose of a body in a lake.'

Jenny expected the detective to look sceptical or cynical when the date was mentioned, but instead she nodded once, and drew a piece of paper from the pile.

'And how old were you both at that time?'

'We were both ten.'

'And you both witnessed this event?' Her pale, almost colourless eyes drilled into Jenny's, who had not yet spoken.

'Yes,' they both replied.

'OK. Now I want you to start from the beginning and tell me everything you remember.'

As Claire retold the story – playing in the grounds of Blackmere Hall, the stakeout, seeing the man carry an object to the jetty, the auburn hair and the splash – Jenny nodded her encouragement.

DI Fielding put down her pen and gave them both a considered stare.

'Why did you not report this earlier?'

'We blocked out the memory. We were too shocked to speak about it that night. The next day my parents came to collect me. And then we went back to communicating by letter... We never spoke about it. It became like something we'd imagined, I suppose, and then we forgot about it completely.'

'How can you be sure now that you didn't imagine the whole thing? Ten-year old girls have very strong imaginations. I have a niece who's about that age. She can tell a very convincing story. You could easily have convinced each other you saw something, and ended up believing your own fantasy.'

'No, we didn't talk about it at all. It started coming back to me only recently, in flashbacks.'

'I see. And why do you think you've started having these flashbacks?'

Claire hesitated. This was the weak point. This would make her look like an unreliable witness. Mentally unstable. Delusional. She looked squarely at the detective and said:

'I've been suffering from depression and seeing a therapist. We talked a lot about my childhood. That's when the memories started coming back.'

The detective raised her eyebrows and wrote something on her paper, then looked up and turned to Jenny. 'And where do you fit in here? Did you remember the events in question?'

'No, not at first. I felt there was something, some bad memory, but it didn't come back to me until we visited Blackmere Hall together. Then I remembered.'

'You remembered everything - the man, the body?'

'Yes,' Jenny lied. She still wasn't one hundred percent sure, but any hesitation now would shut down the whole thing.

'All right. Can you give me a detailed description of the

man, from what you can remember?'

'We can do better than that. I think we've identified him. His name is Tommy Whitaker.'

The detective looked up sharply in surprise. Obviously the name meant something to her.

'And how did you come to that conclusion?' she asked, mildly.

As Claire explained about their drawing of the Caretaker and the photo in the magazine, they could tell from her body language that they were losing DI Fielding. She had stopped writing, and was sitting back in her chair with pursed lips and narrowed eyes.

'It's the scar, you see,' Claire continued in a rush, desperate to regain some control. 'Tommy Whitaker has the same scar. And he bought Blackmere Hall in 1990 when it was almost a ruin. There is a body in that lake. If you dragged it, you would find it. I could tell you exactly where to look. Tommy Whitaker is a criminal. I'm an accountant and I've been looking into his background.' She opened her briefcase and pulled out some papers. 'There are so many financial irregularities. If you look at these documents here, you'll see his income is grossly inflated. I suspect drug trafficking and money laundering...'

She broke off as DI Fielding shook her head with a short laugh and said, not unkindly: 'So, you're a pair of amateur sleuths, are you? And you'd like me to send the frogmen out based on the hazy memories of two ten-year olds?' But she did take the sheaf of papers Claire held out. 'I'll take a look at your papers, of course, but I really don't think there's enough here to launch a full investigation. The police have limited resources, as you know, and we need firm evidence to commit manpower to any case. I'm sorry.' She replaced the cap on her pen and looked at the clock on the wall, signalling that the interview was over.

'Wait! Wait a minute.' Jenny found her voice at last. 'There is more. A string of girls disappeared in the south Leeds area in the nineties. Many of them worked in nightclubs and strip clubs. Tommy Whitaker owned such places at the time. Don't you think there's a connection?'

DI Fielding shrugged. 'It's a sad fact that young girls in certain professions do go missing, I'm afraid. There are many reasons: drug overdoses, suicide, running away to London, for instance. Murder is very rarely the cause of disappearance.' She stood up. 'Now, I will, of course, make a note of everything you have told me. I have your details on file and if anything comes to light you can be sure I will let you know. Here is my card, should you wish to contact me again.' She opened the door and gestured that the two women should leave. 'Thank you very much for talking to me today, and I'm sorry if I disappointed you. Can you make your own way back downstairs?'

They left the building and walked across the paved area leading to the car park. Jenny's shoulders sagged. She was deflated, sheepish.

'I feel like I'm back at school,' she said, 'and we've just been called into the headmistress's office for a royal telling off. I feel about two foot tall.'

But Claire was not feeling small, she was fuming, trembling with rage. 'She didn't listen to a damn thing we said after she found out I'd been depressed. She wrote us off completely. What a fucking waste of time! Well I'm not going to let it drop, I'm not!'

'Claire, I think it's over. We've done all we can. We tried. Don't cry, please!'

Tears of frustration were running down Claire's face and she wiped them away angrily. 'I need a drink,' she said. 'Let's find a pub somewhere and work out a game plan.'

Oh God, thought Jenny, is this never going to end for Claire? Is it turning into an obsession?

***

Later that evening, Paul opened the door cautiously and made his way down the hall to the living room. He found Jenny curled up on the sofa reading her Kindle. She hadn't switched the light on and the room was in semi-darkness. She looked exhausted, her eyes small and her normally rosy complexion grey. He felt a rare rush of tenderness and went to sit next to her, putting an arm round her shoulders.

'Well? Dare I ask? How did you get on today?'

'We were laughed out of court.'

'That bad?'

'Yeah, that bad. The woman detective was perfectly pleasant, but you could tell she couldn't wait to get rid of us. She didn't believe a word.'

'Oh darling... I don't want to say 'I told you so' but...I'm sorry. You poor thing. It must have been a bit of an ordeal, after you'd got your courage up to go.'

Jenny gave a slight smile and shrugged. 'Yes, well, it even sounded ridiculous to me, too, as we were retelling it. I'm not that surprised.'

'So nothing's going to come of it?'

'No, I think it's going to be filed under 'bin'. She gave us the spiel, you know, if anything comes to light, blah, blah, blah. And look, she's given us her business card! Isn't that nice?' She held up the card with an ironic flourish, then flicked it onto the coffee table.

'What about your friend Claire? Was she upset?'

'No, that's the thing. She's furious. She doesn't want to stop there. She was talking about hiring a private investigator.' She looked at Paul with the ghost of a mischievous smile. 'She asked if we'd contribute. Fifty-fifty. What do you think? You up for that?'

At this, Paul pulled away with a horrified expression, mouth agape, ready to protest, and Jenny giggled. 'Don't worry, I'm teasing. I knew you'd hate that idea, and I was non-committal. I just let her blow off steam on the way back home. She needed it. I don't see the point of doing anything else now. I just want to forget about the whole thing.'

'Phew! You really had me going there. Well, I can't say I'm not relieved this is all over. I suggest that if she rings again, you say firmly but gently that you want to drop the whole thing. It's time to get back to normal life. Let me pour us both a glass of wine. Did you have time to cook, or shall I rustle up something?'

'You?'

'Yes, me! Don't look so shocked. I used to cook all the time! I can still make a decent omelette!'

Wow, thought Jenny. Why is he being so nice all of a sudden?

***

DI Fielding tidied her desk and reached for her coat. It had been a long day and she was tired. As she picked up her bag and left the open-plan office, she noticed the light still on in the Chief Inspector's office. On impulse she knocked on the door.

'Come!'

DI Fielding masked her irritation. She hated the affected way he said 'Come' instead of 'Come in'. She opened the door and saw DCI Hardcastle sitting at his desk, looking down at an array of crime scene photos. He was a portly man, overfond of his food and, she suspected, the bottle. He didn't look up as she crossed the floor.

'Have you got a minute, Guv?' she asked.

'Yes, if it's literally one minute.' He glanced up briefly. 'Sit down. What's on your mind?'

'I just wanted to run something by you. It's probably nothing, but something keeps snagging in my mind.'

'Go on.'

'Two women came to see me today. In their early forties, smart, middle-class, well-spoken. They both claim they witnessed a murder when they were ten years old.'

Hardcastle did a quick calculation. 'That's over thirty years ago. Too long to waste our time with, I'd say.' He still hadn't looked up, intent on rearranging the photos on his desk. 'What's bothering you?'

'They said they identified the murderer as Tommy Whitaker, the businessman.'

The Chief Inspector's eyebrows shot up. He dropped the photo he was holding, pushed his chair back a few inches and looked at her properly for the first time. 'Tommy Whitaker? That's ridiculous. I know the man. Decent chap.'

'Really? It's just... I used to work out of Leeds South when I was a young WPC. I was on the beat in the Beeston area quite a bit. And I do remember the name Tommy Whitaker used to come up from time to time. There were some suspicions about him.'

'Nonsense. He's a hardworking chap, that's all, built up an empire from the bottom up. Yes, it's true he started off with nightclubs, but he owns some of the best hotels in Yorkshire now. He's very well connected. My advice is to drop it.'

'OK sir, I just wondered...'

'Look, I play golf with the fellow, for goodness sake. I can vouch for him. Good man, decent as they come. Now, was there anything else?'

'No, Guv.'

'Well, goodnight then.'

The Chief Inspector lifted his considerable bulk from his chair and accompanied her to the door. As she was about to leave, he put a hand on her arm and said: 'But put a copy of your report on my desk will you? I'll have a glance over it in the morning. Put your mind at rest.'

He watched Inspector Fielding make her way down the corridor. He closed the door, thought for a minute, then dug his mobile phone out of his pocket. He searched through his contacts then pressed the green button.

'Tommy? How are you, old chap? Fancy a round of golf this week?'

13

Claire couldn't take her eyes off the photo. She'd stared at it for at least fifteen minutes. Her hands were balled into fists and she felt the bile rise in her throat as she took in the details. She knew she should protect herself, shut down the PC and do something else, something physical, to break the spell. Instead she tortured herself, knowingly, cruelly.

She was mesmerized by the tiny fingers, the exquisite pearly fingernails, the way the delicate pink flesh gripped so tightly around the rougher adult forefinger. Mike's finger. Mike's baby. It was a tasteful photo in black and white. Beautiful, subtle – and it hurt like a bullet to the heart.

She looked at the impressive number of 'Likes' on the Facebook post again, and then dragged the mouse down to read the comments. His parents. His sisters, all ecstatic. She'd loved his family, at one time. In a former life. Now they were as distant as ghosts. And then, oh no, all the friends that used to be mutual! They're all on his side, they're all so happy for him, she realised. She was isolated, cut off, completely alone. She knew it was partly her fault; she'd been too proud to vent her feelings and rage to their friends at the time of the split. Instead she'd kept a dignified silence, hoping people would respect her for her fairness and discretion. Now she realised her mistake. He'd pulled them all over to his side, given his version of the story. How stupid she'd been. He was now in pole position; beautiful young girlfriend, new-born child, large circle of friends. What did she have? She was left stranded on the grid, tank empty. She felt rejected, worthless, powerless.

She'd fought so hard, so long, to resist the old black wave, but now she could feel it behind her back. A tidal wave, huge, powerful, roaring with menace, building up higher and higher, closer and closer, threatening any moment to submerge her and take her down, down into the depths.

It's not fair, it's not fair, she screamed silently. Why does he get to have everything? What have I ever done to be punished like this? Why is life so fucking, fucking shit? Desperately she fought to hold off the wave. I can't go there again, she panicked, I'll never survive it a second time. But she could feel it coming for her, relentlessly.

Finally, she tore her eyes away and slammed the laptop shut. She took a deep breath, and wandered over to the window. It was raining, but she had to get out, go for a long walk, go for a run, try to outrun the wave. She looked at the street below and noticed the car again. Same one. It had been there for the last week, on and off. Always parked on the opposite side of the road. Black, with dark tinted windows making it impossible to see if anyone was inside. Am I being paranoid? she thought. Am I being watched? She pulled the phone from its holder and dialled Jenny's number.

'Jenny, hi, it's Claire. Am I disturbing you?'

'Of course not!' said Jenny, happily. 'You got me at a good time. The boys have just been delivered to school. Paul did it! That's a minor miracle! I didn't even have to ask him. He must be feeling guilty about something. Flowers last week too! What has he done, I wonder? But I'm waffling. How are you?'

'Er, not so great today, actually. A bit blue.'

'Really?' Jenny's tone changed instantly. 'How can I help? Look, I'm not doing anything important today. I can come over for an hour or so, if you like.'

'Um, that's really nice of you. But no, it's raining. Come over on a good day.'

'Why don't you phone your therapist, talk to him?'

'Yes, yes, I'll do that, maybe.'

Jenny could tell from her voice that she was being fobbed off. Claire had not the least intention of phoning her therapist.

'Talk to me!' she said. 'What's on your mind?'

'Oh, general blues. I kept things at bay when we were busy chasing Tommy Whitaker. Now that's gone quiet, things have started to crowd back in again. I don't know... I'm just feeling a bit down.'

'Claire, I'm really sorry I didn't want to carry on with it all. I know how important it is to you. Sorry I didn't want to hire that investigator you found.'

'Oh, don't worry about that. I understand. And I'm still doing a bit of research. Trying to trace relatives of the missing girls online. But listen, I just wanted to, um... to warn you about something... You're going to think I've completely lost the plot... But I think I'm being followed.'

'Followed? Really? When? How?' Jenny tried hard to keep the scepticism from her voice.

'Well, when I go out I just get this feeling, as if someone's watching me. Classic hairs on the back of my neck feeling. And this big black car has been parked up outside quite often. It's got tinted windows. No-one has tinted windows these days, do they? Except drug dealers! I'm not sure it's even legal.'

'Have you seen anyone coming in or out of the car?'

'No, never. I've watched it for hours.'

'Are you really worried?'

'I don't know! Sometimes I think I'm just going crazy!'

'Look, take down the numberplate and phone that detective, DI Fielding. Have you still got her card? Put it on record.

She can trace it and then put your mind at rest.'

'No, I'm not speaking to her after last time. She wouldn't do anything. Oh God. Do *you* think I'm going mad?'

'No, of course not. Look, hold on. I'm coming over. On Saturday. Can you hold on 'til then? We'll go out for the day. Go to Formby beach or somewhere. Oh yeah, Formby! We used to go there with your mum and dad. Do you remember? We can have a long walk and a long talk. Eat fish and chips and make sandcastles even.' Jenny had a vivid memory of racing along the enormous stretch of sand with Claire when they'd been younger, laughing and attempting to cartwheel, as Claire's parents followed at a steadier pace with deckchairs and a picnic basket. She felt suddenly nostalgic for those lost carefree days. Everything had been so uncomplicated back then. Happiness attainable so easily. A sunny day, a chocolate biscuit, a friend...

'Yes, OK. Let's do that.,' Claire agreed. 'That would be really nice. Um, I'm really sorry to worry you.'

'Don't be daft! We're friends! That's what friends are for! I'm so glad we've got back together again. I don't know why we lost touch, it was stupid. But Claire, it's really great to be so close again now. So call me any time if you're feeling low, will you?'

'OK, I will.'

'Promise? I mean it!'

'Promise.'

There was a pause. Then Claire added:

'Jen, but just in case, you take care. Be careful. Keep your eyes open.'

'Don't worry, I will. Bye Claire. See you on Saturday.'

'Bye.'

Claire put the phone back in its cradle, feeling slightly better. Maybe time does heal all, she thought. In a year or two I won't feel this way. It's just a low spot. Everything passes, eventually. She fetched her coat from the cupboard in the hall, laced up her trainers and left the flat. She stared defiantly at the black car as she passed it. It's just a car, she thought, nothing more, as she walked purposefully down the road towards the canal.

If she had turned back to look, she would have seen a figure emerge from the car. A powerfully-built man wearing dark glasses, in spite of the rainy day. If she had looked back, she would have seen the man fall into step several metres behind her, his soft soles silent on the pavement. If she had looked back, she would have chosen another route, one with shops and people and noise. Instead she chose the narrow corridor of the Rochdale Canal, with its steep-sided brick walls leading down to the greenish-black water below.

She strode out purposefully along the towpath, soothed by the peace of the early morning, watching the raindrops cast little ripples on the surface of the water. Gradually the towpath became yet narrower as it passed between the high, blackened walls of factory buildings. A sense of unease gripped her; it was gloomy and enclosed here. She quickened her pace. In a few hundred metres she would reach the more open section with its pretty border of trees and attractive bridges. Suddenly she heard a twig snap behind her. Close behind. Adrenalin kicked in and her body tensed to run. But it was too late. An arm shot out and caught the hood of her coat, forcing her to jerk back and stumble. The arm gripped her viciously tight, as a second arm reached towards her mouth. Then all went black.

If only she'd looked back...

14

DI Fielding was puzzled. Despite a heavy workload, her thoughts kept coming back to Tommy Whitaker. She didn't have time for this. Five urgent case files lay on her desk. She had three witness statements to organise, the crime scene unit to chase up, reports to write. She was falling behind, and it looked as if she'd be working late yet again. She was coming towards the end of her career, and knew she would not get any further up the ladder. But she prided herself on being quietly efficient, dogged, thorough. She hated loose ends, and something about the two women's visit was nagging at her.

She sighed and pushed the heavy files on her desk to one side, reaching instead for a slim sheaf of papers, stapled together at the corner. She once again read the information which Claire had condensed onto the pages. She shook her head. There was not quite enough here. She couldn't send this to the National Crime Agency, or even to HM Customs. For a start, it was impossible to do so without DCI Hardcastle finding out. And he had been formal; there was to be no poking around in Tommy Whitaker's past. And besides, these types of financial investigations tended to take years.

Suddenly she had an idea. She couldn't really afford the time… but damn it, if she got an answer, one way or another, at least she'd be able to concentrate on her current files again. She fetched her coat and crossed the open-plan office to the door, walked very quietly along the corridor, down the stairs, and out to her car.

Half an hour later, she pulled up outside the Park View Retirement Village. It was an impressive development; a cluster of small, modern apartments huddled around a restored Georgian manor house, all set in glorious parkland. Not a bad place to end up, she thought. She'd expected something much more utilitarian and institutional. This was more like a hotel. She made her way to the reception in the main building, and asked for directions to Mr. Healey's apartment.

'It's number eleven, on the left hand side of the drive,' said the receptionist. 'But at this time of the afternoon you'll probably find him on the bowling green. It's behind the main building, past the tennis court.'

Bloody hell! Bowling greens and tennis courts. I'll be lucky to get one room and a colour TV if I ever have to go into a home, she thought, without rancour. He'd been a good bloke, a supportive and hard-working boss, and she didn't begrudge him the luxury of his golden years.

She found him sitting on a bench, leaning forward, watching the game unfold.

'Hello, Guv! Remember me?' she asked.

Ex Chief Inspector Healey pushed his glasses further up his nose and gave her the once-over. He was much smaller and thinner than she remembered him. His hair was shockingly sparse over his liver-spotted scalp. His hands were gnarled and shaky, joined together round the knobbly top of a walking stick. His eyes, however, hadn't lost their sharpness.

'Well, well, well, if it isn't little WPC Angela Fielding. Well I never. It is nice to see you! Come and sit down. What brings you out to visit an old crock like me?'

'Goodness! There's nothing wrong with your memory! I'm impressed you still know my name. And you're not a crock at all. You look in great form to me.' She gestured to the well-kept surroundings. 'You've fallen on your feet here! This place is a palace!'

'I have, haven't I? And before you start asking yourself if I was on the take, the answer's no. My wife had money, you see. I'm very lucky. Come and sit down.' He gestured to the space beside him. 'Tell me what's become of you. Are you a DCI now?'

'No. Couldn't stand all the politics and brown-nosing! I'm just plain old DI. But that's the way I like it. At the sharp end, attempting to solve crime.'

'And have you got a fella? Kids?'

'No. No, that never happened. But my sister's got two kids and I'm a wonderful auntie.'

'This job is hard on relationships. I've seen that time and again. I don't know how my wife used to put up with me. Maybe you're better off single. So how is policing? I suppose things have changed a lot since my day?'

'Oh, you wouldn't believe it, sir. It's not the same job at all. There's loads more paperwork. Everything's got to be in triplicate. And you sit at your computer most of the day. There's lots more technology of course. CCTV, GPS tracking. It's not all bad. I do miss the old days though.'

'So, to what do I owe the honour of this visit? I expect you've come to pick my brains.'

'I have indeed.'

'Is it to do with an investigation?'

'Not exactly. There's no case, as such. But a name has come up that I think you might remember. I wanted to get your impression of the man.'

'All right. Fire away. Who is this man?'

'Tommy Whitaker.'

'Ah.' The old man sat back in his seat and nodded slowly. 'I see.'

DI Fielding waited, as Healey collected his thoughts.

'Is he suspected of a crime, or has he been the victim?'

'I have two very unreliable witnesses that suspect him of disposing of a body, many years ago. And I'm not sure how seriously to take it. There were rumours about him back then, weren't there?'

'Oh yes. More than rumours. But we could never pin anything on him.'

'Was it drug trafficking?'

'Yes, probably. And worse.'

'Worse?'

Healey sighed and leaned forward once again. 'I had a very strong indication that he was organising sex parties. Not very pleasant ones. He invited his cronies, people he wanted to blackmail, people who could help him... Drugs were taken... and young women were abused.'

'I see! But you never had proof?'

Healey looked away, his expression sad. 'I had an informant. Young woman, prostitute. Delightful girl. She used to point out the drug runners and such. One day I saw her on the street, pulled her over and she got into the car. Her face was a mess. Broken nose, smashed ribs, she said she had cigarette burns on her thighs. She told me she'd been forced to go to one of Tommy's parties. She'd been abused by a group of men. There were other rooms, other girls. I begged her to come in and make a statement, but she was terrified. She wouldn't press charges. She kept saying 'He'll kill me.' She wouldn't speak to me after that.'

'What was her name?'

'Tessa. Damn it, I can't remember her surname. It was something foreign. Italian or Spanish, I think'

'So, what do you think? Is he someone capable of murder?'

'Murder?' The old man nodded, thoughtfully. 'Yes, I suppose he might be.'

'Thanks, sir. Thank you so much for your time. You've been a great help.' She got up to leave, but he laid a trembling hand on her arm.

'Wait a minute. I've kept all my old notes. I'll look through them and see what I can find. Write down my phone number.' He recited the digits carefully. 'Call me again in a couple of days.'

'OK, I will. Thank you.'

'But Angela, a word of warning. The man has got friends in all sorts of places. Maybe even on the force. Keep this all to yourself for now.'

'I will.' She smiled and impulsively leant across to give him a kiss on the cheek.

'Bye, Guv.'

15

'Stop pacing around' said Paul. 'Sit down, for Christ's sake!'

'I can't settle. I'm worried.'

'I think you're being over-dramatic. She's either lost her phone or dropped it down the loo or something. Bound to be a logical explanation.'

'But she's got a landline too, and she's not answering that either.'

'Come and sit down.' He patted the sofa beside him and turned again to the TV.

'But we were supposed to meet up tomorrow and go to the beach. We haven't arranged a time, or if we're meeting at the beach or at her flat. It's not like her. I *am* worried!'

'Maybe she's had second thoughts and doesn't want to go.'

'No. She was quite depressed when we spoke. She said she had the blues. I should have asked her more about how she was feeling. Got her to open up a bit more. Instead I just told her to speak to her therapist. I hope she's OK. I think I should ring her mum and dad.'

'Is that a good idea? You might make them worried too, when there's no reason.'

But Jenny had already grabbed the phone. She called her own parents, had a brief chat, and asked for Ken and Dora Hasting's telephone number. Then she dialled.

Paul gave an exaggerated sigh and started to flip through the channels as she spoke, but gradually he began to notice that Jenny had gone more and more quiet. He glanced over at her. She was sitting, frozen on the chair, staring into the garden with unseeing eyes. The phone was grasped tightly in one hand, the other hand was held over her mouth. He listened, intrigued. Jenny was responding in short monosyllables as the person on the other end talked:

'Oh ... Oh no! ... Oh my God! ... When did it...? .... Oh God! ... Yes ... Yes, only three days ago ... Yes, she was .... She said she was feeling down ... Oh Christ ... Where did they take her? ... OK ... I'm so sorry for you and Ken ... Let me know what I can do ... OK ... OK ... Thank you ... Goodbye. Bye.'

'What's happened?' asked Paul, switching off the TV and getting up from the sofa.

Jenny was pale and trembling with shock. Her eyes were huge. 'It's Claire. She tried to kill herself. She jumped in the canal.'

'Really? Shit! Is she dead?'

'No, she's not dead. There was a couple walking by. They saw her in the water and managed to pull her out.'

'Well, thank goodness. Is she injured?'

'I don't know. Um, they had to give her mouth-to-mouth, apparently. And when she came round she was hysterical, incoherent. The couple called an ambulance. I guess they took her to hospital, but she's ended up back in the psychiatric hospital where she was before. Oh God! Poor Claire!'

Paul put his arms around her and hugged her, one hand stroking the hair at the back of her head. He rocked her gently from side to side.

'Shh. Don't cry. She's in the best possible place now. They'll look after her there.'

'It's so awful, Paul! Dora said that her ex-husband had posted a photo of his new baby on social media that same morning. She must have seen it. It must have tipped her over the edge.'

'Poor girl, that's rough.'

'It was the same day she phoned me. Why didn't she tell me? I could have helped. I would have gone over there...'

'Don't blame yourself. Maybe she didn't want to burden you with it.'

'And Dora and Ken were allowed to visit just briefly. They said she was just staring into space, didn't seem to recognise them or even try to talk to them.'

'I think that's probably normal. She'll be heavily sedated for a while. Don't worry, she'll get better.'

Jenny gulped for air as the sobs overtook her. 'It's my fault! It's all my fault!'

Paul gave her a gentle shake. 'Don't be silly. It's not your fault. Sit down.' He led her back to the sofa and gently pressed her down onto the cushions. 'I'm just going to pour you a whisky. Stay there.'

He came back moments later with a large shot of Highland Park, and folded her shaking hands round the glass. 'Drink this. Big gulp. There you go. Now, listen to me. You know Claire tried to kill herself once before, don't you?'

'Yes.'

'And it's a horrible fact that people who attempt suicide once often try again.'

'Yes, but...'

'There was nothing you could do to prevent it. If people make their minds up, you can't stop them.'

'But I didn't support her enough. I didn't back her up enough about the murder. And I didn't talk to her enough about how she was feeling.'

'Nonsense. You were a great friend to her. You went over and above the call to help her with the murder mystery. Not everyone would have done that. And listen: she's not dead! She will recover and she will be fine! Do you want me to drive you over to visit her?'

Jenny was touched by his concern. This was the Paul of old, caring and supportive. She gave him a brave smile. 'Thanks, but we're not allowed, it seems. No visitors until they've 'stabilised' her, whatever that means. I don't know how long that will be.'

They sat together on the sofa all evening, talking and holding each other, Jenny crying again from time to time, Paul comforting her as best he could.

That night, they made love, for the first time in a while. Jenny knew that she'd been too tired or too irritable to initiate sex much of late, but that night was different. She was desperate for the warmth of another body, for contact, for the affirmation of life and love and hope. She clung to Paul and he responded with equal ardour. For those few minutes, she felt sweet release and uncomplicated joy. All the tension left her body. Then it was over. Paul fell asleep immediately, but Jenny couldn't find rest. As the hours ticked away, she went over and over in her mind all the conversations she'd had with Claire since that very first phone call, and all the hints that she could have missed.

Was it really the ex-husband's fault? Was it the baby photo? Or had she let her friend down? Had she accidentally said something hurtful? Had she missed some cries for help?

Or was it just possible that Claire really had been followed?

16

DI Fielding was taking no chances. She went out to the car park and glanced round to make sure no-one was within earshot before making the call. Holding her mobile to her chin with her shoulder, she noted down the name he dictated, asking him to double check the spelling. Then she read it back to him:

'Tessa Ungaretti. Thanks, boss. That's great! Do you have any idea where she might be now?'

'She's in the phone book. I checked.' He gave her the number. 'It's a very unusual name, so I'm guessing it's the same girl. Or woman, should I say. She'll be in her fifties now. If you speak to her, tell her I was asking after her, and hope she managed to make a good life for herself.'

'I will. Thanks for all your help, boss. Now, get back to your bowls and forget all about it! I'll come and visit you again when it's all over, if I may.'

Healey chuckled and said goodbye.

Fielding took a moment to plan her approach, then dialled the number.

'Hello.' A deep male voice, gruff and unwelcoming.

'Hello. Can I speak to Tessa, please?'

'Who's this?'

'It's Angela.' She didn't give her last name or rank. She hoped he'd assume she was an old friend. 'Just calling for a chat.'

'Tessa!' he yelled. 'It's for you!'

'Hello?' A female voice this time, tired, unfriendly.

'Is that Tessa?'

'Yeah, that's me. Who are you?' This time DI Fielding heard the strong Yorkshire accent.

'My name's Angela. I'm a friend of DCI Healey, do you remember him?'

There was a pause at the other end. Then a cautious 'What d'you want?'

'I just wanted to ask you a couple of questions about the past. It won't take a minute. I really need your help.'

'What about?' The voice was now openly hostile, suspicious.

'It's about someone you knew in the past. I'm looking for information about Tommy Whitaker. I think….'

That was as far as she got. Tessa Ungaretti had cut the connection. Fielding dialled again, but this time there was no reply. With a sigh, she went back into the station and sat at her desk in the open-plan office once more, concentrating on her case files. A couple of hours later, she went out to try again. No answer. Then for a third time she left her seat.

'What's up wi' you?' asked her colleague, Tony. 'You started smokin' or sommat? You're up and down like a whore's drawers today!'

'Don't be a dick, Tony. Just off to the ladies.'

Checking the cubicles were all empty, with doors wide open, she stood facing the entrance and dialled a third time, and this time Tessa answered.

'Hello.'

'Please don't hang up! It's Angela again. Please just listen for one minute!'

'I 'aven't got time for this.'

'Wait, please! Just one minute. I swear I won't involve you in anything, whatever you say will be totally off the record. Your name will never be mentioned. But I really need your help.'

'I've got nowt to say.'

'OK, OK. Wait! Don't go! I tell you what. I'll do all the talking. You say nothing. Just say Yes or No, if I'm on the right track. OK?'

'You a copper, then?'

'Yes. But you can trust me. I'm one of the good guys. Like Healey was. He was asking after you. He cared about you.'

Another long pause. 'Go on, then. Say your piece.'

'Right, thank you, Tessa. Thanks so much. I'm looking at Tommy Whitaker's past. I have two witnesses who've accused him of murder. I'm trying to find out what he was into about thirty years ago.'

'Go on.'

'He had nightclubs, strip joints, nail bars and pizza places, is that right?'

'Yes.'

'And he was supplying drugs, is that correct?'

This time a pause, then a reluctant 'Yes.'

'I think he also held parties for male friends. Young women were drugged and abused. Am I right?'

'Yes.' This time the voice was small, almost a whisper.

DI Fielding took a leap into speculation with her next question:

'And I think a young woman connected to Whitaker disappeared. Is that right?'

Seconds passed. Fielding was about to repeat the question when Tessa answered:

'No.'

'Oh, OK then....' Fielding was disappointed, but not too surprised. A regular run-of-the-mill gangster then. Drugs, prostitution... but not necessarily a murderer. Nothing she needed to get involved in. If he hadn't been found guilty of anything back then, it would be too late now. She could put the case out of her mind and get on with her workload. 'Right. So was he...?'

'Not one. At least four. That I know of.'

Fielding gasped. 'Four? Four women disappeared? Is that what you're telling me?

'Yes.' The voice was hardly audible.

'Can you tell me their names?'

'That's all I'm sayin'. Don't phone again.'

'Wait, wait!'

But the line went dead once more. Fielding looked at the mobile phone in her hand, then glanced up and saw her face reflected in the mirror. She saw the shock and disbelief etched onto her features. Four women! That was years in the past. What if he'd carried on? This could be huge!

Where the hell do I go with this? she thought. This is too big for me. Who do I take it to? But it was all still word of mouth. What did she really have? The suspicions of an elderly retired policeman. The memories of two girls who'd been far too young to be trusted as witnesses. And finally, the words of an ex-prostitute, who would, in any case, never agree to testify. It would never hold water. She needed something concrete before jumping over her own boss and taking it to the Chief Superintendent. But would it be possible to continue to investigate without alerting suspicion? And did she really want to open up this can of worms?

DI Fielding walked slowly down the corridor and back to her desk. She threw herself into her case files with extra energy, organising the witness statements and chasing up the crime scene unit. She'd think about it later.

17

Jenny sat at her easel and tried to concentrate on her painting. A dwarf rabbit. Who the hell spends hundreds of pounds on a portrait of a rabbit? she wondered. Admittedly it was a pretty little thing, with enormous black eyes and a tiny button nose. But just a ball of fluff, really, with no discernible character. She was having difficulty finding a focal point for the painting, but plodded on methodically.

The week had passed slowly. Jenny had called either the hospital, or Claire's parents, every day, for updates. She was told the same thing each time: Claire was receiving treatment and the doctors were cautiously optimistic. Her physical and mental symptoms - anxiety, delusion, paranoia, hysteria - were being addressed at the moment with medication. When these started to abate they would begin the talking therapies.

So Jenny immersed herself in her work and her family, helping the boys with homework, cooking elaborate home-made meals and even playing Monopoly, which she hated. Paul continued to be solicitous, and had been making much more effort to help her with the boys. He was still working late each night, but had taken the boys off cycling at the weekend so she could get more painting done. However, each time she found herself inactive, her thoughts always returned to Claire. What could I have done differently? What signs did I miss? she thought, again and again. Will she be OK?

Jenny was about to pack up and start cleaning her

brushes, when the phone rang.

'Good afternoon. Is that Jennifer Kerr?' A male voice, deep, pleasant and musical.

'Yes, speaking.' She assumed it was a potential client, and put on her best business-like voice. Another commission would take her mind off things. A welcome distraction. But not another bloody rabbit, please!

'This is Tommy Whitaker.'

Jenny could not speak. Shock, fear and some degree of embarrassment made the blood rush to her cheeks. She was unable to reply.

The man gave a throaty chuckle. 'I expect that name came as a bit of a shock to you. I *do* apologise. Really, the last thing I want is to worry you. But I was hoping we might have a little chat.'

Jenny remained silent. She could find no words. She wanted to put the phone down, but it seemed she was unable to move.

'Now, *please* don't be angry that I got in touch. I really want to *help* you, you see.' He had a trick of overemphasising certain words that made him sound like a classical actor. Effete, almost effeminate. No trace of an accent. 'I have a friend on the police force, who told me a funny story the other day. He said that two little girls thought they saw me doing a *dastardly deed* way back in the past.' Again he chuckled, as if the whole story was vastly amusing. 'I found it very funny, you see, I *roared* with laughter, but then I started to think: those poor little girls who made a mistake! Those poor grown-up ladies who must still really believe something nasty happened. I realised I had to put the record straight. I couldn't not! What if you were both still worrying your heads about something so *silly*.'

'I um...' Jenny's mouth was dry and she stumbled to a halt.

'Now really, I *promise* I'm not a bogeyman. I'm a very normal chap. I believe I know your father, too! We're on the same committees. He's *delightful*. Very knowledgeable! And I have met your mother on a couple of occasions at various functions. *Such* a lovely lady. So proud of you! So, my dear, I would really like the opportunity to meet you and your friend, to put all these doubts you have to rest. Do you think you might agree to that?'

'Err...um... I'm afraid that's not possible. Claire isn't um... isn't available. I'm sorry, but no.'

'Oh, that *is* a shame. Let me see, now. Might I perhaps invite you and your good husband to lunch, then?'

'No, I...'

'Come to Blackmere Hall. My treat. I can hopefully explain *exactly* what you think you saw, and put your mind *quite* at rest.'

'No! Not Blackmere Hall,' squeaked Jenny, horrified.

'Oh, silly me, of course not. How *stupid*. The scene of my crime!' He laughed delightedly. 'No, no, not there. I would be most happy if you and your husband would care to join me at the restaurant of your choice. Anywhere you choose, my dear. Any time.'

Jenny found herself mesmerised by his voice. It was warm, kindly, full suppressed laughter. He sounded like a benevolent uncle, or a favourite old, possibly gay, teacher. He was cultivated and courteous. Was this really the same man as the 'Caretaker' who had chased them down the steps and sworn at them? Was Claire totally mistaken? But maybe it was all an act, designed to lure her into a trap. Should she agree? If she went to hear his explanation, would it not help Claire? Help her get over her obsession? She couldn't make her mind up. Was it dangerous? But if she went with Paul, nothing could happen surely? And she would know, one way or another...

'I can tell you are in two minds. What can I say to convince you? We'll have a *jolly* good lunch and I will say my piece, and if you don't believe me, that is absolutely fine. I shall go away and leave you in peace. But I do *so* hate misunderstandings.'

Jenny made a decision. They would go. She racked her brains to think of a restaurant which would be full of people, well-lit and with no secluded corners.

'Very well. Do you know the Brewers Arms just off junction twenty-six of the M62?'

'I can't say I know it, my dear, but I'm quite sure my driver can find it. *Splendid.* What day would suit you?'

Why put it off, thought Jenny. 'Tomorrow? Twelve o'clock?' Paul would just have to take a long lunch break. She'd find a way to persuade him.

'That would be perfect. I shall look forward to meeting you *very* much. Goodbye, my dear, and thank you *so* much.'

Jenny put the phone back in its cradle with a shaking hand. She'd been hasty, impulsive.

Oh my God! She thought. What have I done?

***

When she heard Paul's key in the lock that evening, Jenny hurried into the hall to meet him. She hung up his coat and gave him a quick kiss.

'What's the welcoming committee for?' asked Paul, bemused.

She took both his hands in hers, looked into his eyes and asked:

'Paul, will you do something for me? Something important?'

'Yes, if I can. What?'

'Will you come and meet Tommy Whitaker tomorrow

with me?'

'Who's he?'

'Oh, Paul!' she chided, lightly. She was exasperated by his short memory. Just goes to show how seriously he's been taking it all, she thought. But she would not criticise; she needed to keep him onside. There was no way she could face the man alone. 'He's the man at Blackmere Hall, the one...'

'Ah, the body-in-the-lake man! Why do you want to meet him?'

'He phoned me today. He said he could explain everything and that it was all a misunderstanding. I thought it would help Claire if I heard him out. But I don't want to go alone. I still think he might be dangerous.'

Paul thought for a moment. He couldn't really spare the time, but on the other hand, if this meeting managed to put the whole thing to bed, things could finally go back to normal. That was what he wanted more than anything. This murder nonsense had been a bore, and Jenny had been different lately, distracted and distant. The sooner it went away, the better.

'Well... OK. I guess I can come with you, if it doesn't take too long. Where does he want to meet?'

'I suggested lunch at the Brewers at midday. It's always busy there, so he can't, you know, kidnap us at gunpoint or stab us or anything. It's weird, Paul, he sounded really nice on the phone. Friendly. Normal. I'm really confused.'

'Well, in that case, it's a good thing we're meeting him. Everything will be clearer after tomorrow.' He gave her two hands a squeeze, then let them drop. 'Now, where are the boys? Is it too late for a bedtime story?'

'No, they're still mucking about up there, I can hear them. Go on up and I'll get the dinner ready. And Paul...?'

'Yeah?'

'Thanks. You're a star.'

He kissed the top of her head, then put on his Jack Nicholson crazy face from *The Shining* and raced up the stairs, calling out in a fake-creepy voice: 'Oh Jakey! Oh Davie! Daddy's home!'

'Idiot!' said Jenny, fondly, and went into the kitchen. He *is* a good man, she thought. He does support me when it counts. They had been getting on better and better, oddly, since Claire's 'accident'. There was more physical contact, more conversation, and he was definitely making an effort to share some of the household chores. She'd been careful to ask him occasionally about his work too, although she found herself switching off when he went into detail.

She smiled to herself as she opened the fridge. They would face Tommy Whitaker together, as a united couple. She wasn't alone now. Between the two of them, they would work out exactly what kind of a man he was, and what action they needed to take.

18

Claire's slender body twitched and spasmed as she slept. She dreamt she was in the water, her heavy clothes pulling her down, down, her arms flailing uselessly as the murky water entered her nose and mouth. Her head was throbbing from a blow. Stay conscious, stay awake! But her head was now slipping under the water, and as she fought to regain the surface, she could see a shimmering dark form, immobile, looking down at her, impassively. She was going to die. She couldn't die! No, no, no, no, no!

Claire's head thrashed about on the pillow and she started to shout, then scream:

'Help! Help me! Help me!'

The door burst open and a nurse appeared, rushing over to the bed and laying a soothing hand on her arm.

'Calm down, Claire. You're OK. Take deep breaths.'

Claire batted the hand away angrily and struggled to sit up.

'Let me go! I've got to get out! He tried to kill me! I've got to warn her!' Her voice was shrill and her pulse was racing alarmingly.

The nurse gently put both hands on Claire's shoulders to ease her back onto the pillows, but Claire resisted, thrashing out wildly and catching the nurse squarely on the jaw.

'Doctor! Doctor! Room 12 please!' called the nurse, calmly, whilst discretely pressing the staff attack button on her badge. She continued to talk in a low, soothing voice but her grip was firm. 'You're OK, Claire. Just lie still. You've had a shock. You're in hospital. You're going to be OK.'

Then the doctor entered the room. Claire continued to struggle and scream as he took her pulse.

'Fuck off! Let me go! She's in danger! Let me... leh...'

Her voice trailed off as the injection took hold. She felt her arms and legs start to tingle, almost pleasantly. The world began to slow down around her. The doctor's face was blurred and his voice was coming from far, far away. She tried to push him away but her arm was sluggish, useless, it wouldn't obey her. Her legs were now heavy as lead. She tried vainly to lift her right leg off the bed but found she couldn't move it at all. There was something important she had to do, but she could no longer remember what it was. Think! Then her memory shut down. She smiled, dreamily, as her heart rate slowed down. Her breathing deepened and her eyelids started to close. Sleep. Sleep. That's what I need. Everything will be OK if I sleep.

19

Paul and Jenny sat at a round table in the bay window, overlooking the entrance. From the outside, the pub-restaurant was generically bland, with its large windows and a fake-Tudor façade. Inside the orange carpet was surprisingly brash and a neon sign on the wall urged them to Eat, Drink and Relax. Jenny scanned the car park nervously every few seconds. Paul looked at his watch again. It was not yet midday, but he hoped the guy would not be late. He had things to do.

A big black car crawled slowly towards the front of the restaurant and stopped right outside the door. Tinted windows, thought Jenny. Just like Claire said. Are they even legal? The driver's door opened and a man stepped out. He was broad shouldered, stocky. His hair was cut very short and he wore opaque sunglasses and a black suit which strained against his chest. Christ, thought Jenny, he looks like a bouncer outside a seedy nightclub! That can't be him! Can it? Too young surely. In his forties. He looks a bit sinister, though. But the man walked round to the rear door and opened it. A smart brown leather brogue appeared, then another, and finally this second man fully emerged. Jenny noticed the suit first; sky-blue tweed with a white pinstripe, flashy, ostentatious. The body it encased was tall and overweight, with a sizeable paunch. And finally the head; fleshy, jowly. The scar that half-closed one eye was a white streak in an otherwise florid complexion. And then the hair; it was obviously dyed, a sandy-red colour, unlikely for a man in his sixties. All in all, he looked faintly ridiculous, like an un-wanted wedding guest with terrible dress sense. But he carried himself with enormous self-confidence as he walked towards the restaurant. There was something rather magnificent about him.

'Is that your man?' asked Paul.

'Yes, that's him. He's got the scar over his eye.'

'He looks about as threatening as a teddy-bear!' Paul scoffed. 'I think you can stop tearing that beer mat up now.'

Jenny looked down in surprise at the mass of shredded cardboard next to her glass. She swept it quickly into her open handbag and then took a large, reassuring gulp of wine.

'Well, hello there!' That voice again, deep, full of warmth. 'You must be Jennifer?' She remained seated, silent. Unper-turbed, he reached over to shake her hand. 'And you must be Mr Kerr?'

'Yes, I'm Paul Kerr.' Paul half-stood and gave a firm hand-shake.

'Now, let me get you both another drink. What are you having?'

Paul ordered another half of bitter but Jenny refused. You can't buy me that easily, she thought. She watched the man stride off to the bar, lean over and give his order, instantly com-manding the attention of the bar staff. Out of the corner of her eye she saw the other man, the chauffeur, slip into the restaur-ant and place himself discretely at the far end of the bar. Even though he'd kept his sunglasses on, she could tell he was looking at her, steadily. Something about this man made her flesh creep.

'Now then,' said Tommy Whitaker, placing the glasses on the table and taking a seat. He beamed across at them both, to-tally at ease. 'I must say how *nice* it is to meet you, Jennifer. Your parents often talk about you. And I must confess I looked you up on the internet. You are a *most* talented artist. Where did you go to art school?'

Jenny's hackles rose. This man was trying too hard, being too false. 'I didn't,' she answered, shortly. Paul gave her a disapproving look and she glared back at him. Don't be taken in, she begged him silently.

Whitaker caught the look that passed between them and it seemed to amuse him. He chuckled softly.

'Well now, I suggest we clear the air before we order lunch. Then we can all enjoy a jolly good meal. What do you say?' He smiled across at them in turn. 'So my dear, I understand that you and your friend saw me chuck something into the lake at Blackmere Hall. You thought it was a body. Am I correct?'

'That's right.' She returned his gaze with a stony expression.

'And that would be in about 1990, if I'm not mistaken. Let me see… I bought Blackmere Hall in the July of that year. It was my first big purchase. I was *so* proud of it! But my *goodness*, it was in a state! I don't know if you remember much about the place, but it had been empty for years. Very neglected. My first job was to try and clear out all the rubbish that had been left inside. My *goodness*, the things that the last people had left! Hideous paintings, mouldy fabrics, broken chairs. It was *such* a mess. These days I would just call in a team of house clearers and get them to do the lot, but in those days, you see, I didn't have much money. So I was a bit naughty.' He laughed, looking down at his hands with a sheepish expression. 'I didn't bother hiring a van and taking things to the tip. The nearest centre was miles away. I was very bad. I used to carry things down to the rowing boat and row out a little way into the lake, then throw them in. Or with bulky things like chairs, I stood at the end of a little jetty and threw them as far as I could. Wheelbarrow-loads of broken tiles and floorboards went in. If you looked in the bottom of that lake now you'd see all sorts of rubbish, but probably some ancient treasures too.' He looked earnestly at Jenny, but she remained stony-faced.

'I know, I know, it was *very* bad of me. Nowadays you sort your rubbish and recycle or upcycle things, and that's exactly how it should be. I'm sure there was a lot that could have been saved. But I was an impatient young man. I didn't have time for all that.' His expression was now contrite. 'So, tell me, Jennifer, what did you and your friend see, exactly?'

Jenny kept her gaze level as she spoke. 'We saw you carry a rolled up carpet to the rowing boat. It was heavy. When you were in the boat you stumbled. You almost dropped the roll. And we saw long brown hair fall out of one end. It was a body.' She thought she saw him flinch ever so slightly at the word 'body'. Or was she imagining it? The expression was instantly replaced by a wide smile.

'Oh my, oh my!' Again that little chuckle. 'A body! Well, I really don't know about that, but, my gosh, there were certainly lots of carpets and rugs to throw away. And curtains too. Oh, those rugs! I can still remember the smell of them! Mouldy, damp, covered in mouse droppings and crawling with wood-lice. So, are you absolutely sure, dear, that you saw some hair? Can you be positive about that?'

Jenny hesitated. It was Claire who was convinced about the hair, and she herself was not at all sure. She could picture it clearly in her mind, the brown hair swaying in the breeze, the rowing boat rocking as he shifted the load in his arms. But had she invented the image? Had she filled in the gaps in her own memory using Claire's words? Or was the memory her own? Whatever the truth was, it would be disloyal to Claire to admit her doubts to this insufferably pompous man, though. She decided to lie, brazenly.

'I'm sure.'

'Even though you were a very little girl at the time? Could you have imagined that?'

'No.'

'Ah, I see. Let me think.' He paused, and Jenny was transfixed by the frown which only touched half of his face. 'Yes, right. There is one possible explanation I can think of. Curtains. I can remember throwing away some ancient gold-coloured silk curtains. Maybe I rolled the carpet around them. Do you see? If they were tucked inside the roll of carpet, they may have slipped out. Silk curtains could look a little like hair, don't you think? That's the only thing I can think of. Could that be it?'

He gazed at Jenny, one eyebrow now raised in enquiry, the other one curiously immobile, anchored in place by the scar. He looked almost comical, but at the same time repulsive. Jenny felt on the verge of hysterical nervous laughter, but managed to keep her voice level.

'I don't think so,' she said. 'We were sure it was hair.'

'And what do you think, Mister Kerr?' He turned to Paul. 'You are an impartial bystander. What's your understanding of all this?'

Paul was torn. He wanted very much to back up his wife, but he had never given a moment's credence to the murder theory. He was about to share this opinion when he caught Jenny glaring at him balefully, so instead just said, blandly: 'I really couldn't say.'

'Well then. I suppose we shall never get to the bottom of this little mystery. But I'm *most* glad to have contributed a little more information to your puzzle.' He gave Jenny a fatherly smile that infuriated her. Condescending prat, she thought. Puzzle! Did he think of it as a game? Some kind of murder mystery weekend where you work out the clues and nominate the baddie? But as she looked at him, she thought how clever he was being. He was creating the impression of an elderly, bumbling, old-fashioned and pompous idiot. But what if that was all a pretence? A deliberate charade? Was there steel underneath the harmless façade?

'Now then,' he continued. 'Shall we look at these menus? I

think we all deserve a jolly good lunch now! I do hope they have some old-fashioned puddings, like treacle sponge or apple pie.'

Jenny itched to leave immediately. She had no appetite and didn't want to sit near this odious man for a minute longer. But to her dismay, Paul had reached for the menu and was turning the pages. She tried to catch his eye, in vain.

'I'll have the mixed grill,' said Paul.

'Ah, the mixed gorilla. Ha! Ha! Good choice. And for you, my dear?'

Reluctantly, she picked up her own menu, choosing the first thing she saw.

When Whitaker went up to the bar to order their meals, Jenny gave Paul a smart kick under the table. He looked up in surprise.

'What?'

'I didn't want to stay.' She hissed. 'He's awful! Can we make an excuse and go?'

'No, I'm starving! I need some something to eat before I go back to the office. Come on, it's a free lunch. And he's perfectly harmless.'

'I don't think he is. I think it's all an act. He's a snake under all that false bonhomie.'

'Oh, come on! He's just a pompous old fart. You don't seriously still think he murdered someone?'

'Oh, I don't know. I really don't know. But he's creepy!'

'Well, I tell you what,' Paul said, placatingly, 'we won't have a pudding. We'll make our excuses as soon as we've finished the first course. That won't take long. How's that?'

But it didn't work out that way. Whitaker kept up a stream of small talk as they ate, to which Paul mostly replied. And then he played his trump card:

'So, Mr Kerr, tell me, what is it that *you* do for a living?' he asked, focusing the full warmth of his gaze on Jenny's husband.

'I work in data security.'

'Data security. I'm afraid I have not the faintest idea what that is! Can you explain it to an old dinosaur like me?'

Oh no! Here we go, thought Jenny. We'll be here for ages now. Paul launched into his slightly dumbed-down explanation, and Whitaker leaned forward, appearing fascinated.

'Well, basically, it's making sure that all the data in any business is safe. Everything to do with your assets, your websites, your computers, your databases. They need to be made safe from accidental loss, or from malicious attacks.'

'I see. So, how do you make them safe?'

'Well, if it's a case of accidental loss of data, you create back-ups. But if it's malicious hacking, for example, its more complicated. Take your business. You have a chain of hotels, I believe?'

'Yes, that's right.'

'The hospitality industry is a big target for cyber-criminals. One of your most important assets, I imagine, would be your list of clients, with their phone numbers and credit card numbers, their bank details. That kind of stuff is gold dust to a malicious hacker. They can use the information they gather for identity theft or credit card fraud. There was a major hotel chain back in 2010 which had six hundred thousand of their customers' bank details stolen. You can imagine the damage that causes. Not only to your reputation, but you would also have to pay a hefty fine.'

'Golly! That is all very worrying! So how do you protect the data?'

'Well, first of all, we would encrypt all the credit card information. Then we'd install some state-of-the-art firewalls and anti-malware. We'd train your employees in fraud detection. And we would also try to simulate some hacks, so that we could identify weak points in the system.'

As he continued to talk, Paul became more and more animated. The terms he used were becoming more and more complex too: tokenism, key management, traffic filtering and multiple touchpoints. Whitaker was nodding along enthusiastically, and Jenny's suspicious instincts were on full alert. He knew all about this already, she was sure. He was trying, and succeeding, to win Paul over.

'And your company can do all this work?' Whitaker asked.

'Oh yes. We've worked with some up-and-coming medium-sized companies in the region.' Paul went on to mention two or three of his biggest clients.

'Very impressive. How long have you been in this business?'

'Oh, several years now, but I set up my own company just recently. There's just the two of us, myself and my colleague, Marianne. But you don't need a big staff to do this type of work. Just the right people.'

'How long would it take to completely overhaul the data security in my businesses, for example?'

'Well, that would depend on several factors. I'd need to know a lot more about your business before I could hazard a guess.'

No, no, no, screamed Jenny silently. She could see where this was going.

'My dear man, I am so glad you told me all of this! My chief of security is only a little younger than me, I'm afraid, and *desperately* out of touch. I would be so pleased if we could arrange for you to visit the businesses and give me a quote for the work.' He beamed at Paul, who smiled back, delighted. 'Here is my business card. Please give me call.' He handed over the small card with a flourish. 'Well, this has been a *most* fortuitous meeting, I can't *say* how much I've enjoyed it! Now, shall we order puddings?'

Paul opened his mouth to say something, but another kick from Jenny made him close it again. He looked at her, perplexed.

'Sorry. We can't stay. We're going now,' she said, shortly, earning another disapproving look from Paul. She picked up her bag, stood up and stalked past Whitaker without a glance. Paul was left with no alternative but to follow, but he shook the older man's hand enthusiastically as he said his goodbyes, before hurrying to catch up with his wife.

Jenny was furious. She stormed across the car park with a thunderous expression, then turned her head, ready to round on him. Suddenly she caught sight of something that made her keep her opinions to herself, at least until they were safely inside the car: it was the other man. What exactly was he? A chauffeur? Or was he a henchman? A fixer? He was leaning against the black car with his massive arms folded across his chest. Behind his sunglasses, his expression was impassive. He watched them get into their car, then turned his head, following their progress out of the car park and onto the lane.

'He totally played you!' she exploded, when at last they reached the main road. 'And you fell for it, hook, line and sinker!'

'What? Don't be ridiculous. I played him! I had him eating out of my hand.'

'No. Don't you realise? Oh, he was clever. He wanted to neutralise me by getting you on side.'

'Neutralise you?' Paul gave a snort of laughter. 'What do you think you are, an ace detective? James Bond? An atom bomb? Get real, will you! You are a middle aged housewife with some mixed-up faded memories, and he was kind enough to humour you.'

Jenny was aghast at the venom in his voice. 'Middle-aged housewife' indeed – he knew how much that would hurt. It was dismissive and cruel. Tears came into her eyes and she brushed them away angrily.

'Paul, it was all an act. You must see that!'

'What I saw was a decent old man trying very hard to be kind. I actually felt sorry for the guy. You were unforgivably rude to him.'

'God, I can't believe this! Either you are a dreadful judge of character, or you're so blinded by his money that you just don't care!'

'You're the one who's blinded! Blinded by a misplaced loyalty to your friend – a friend who is in a mental institution, I might add!'

'You are not taking his business!'

'I am, if he offers it.'

'I won't let you!'

'It's not your decision.'

'Paul, if you...'

'I'm not discussing it any more. You need get a grip on reality. We'll talk about it tonight when you've calmed down.' To signal the end of the discussion he switched on the radio and turned up the volume.

Jenny was tempted to snap the radio back off again, but instead she clenched her jaw and her fists, and gazed stonily ahead as the kilometres sped past.

20

Jenny seethed with anger and frustration on the short drive home. When Paul stopped the car in front of their house, she got out wordlessly and stalked toward the front door without a backward glance. Paul didn't notice though; he was already reversing down the drive.

Trembling with suppressed emotion, she threw her coat and bag in the hall and ran up the stairs. She sat for a long moment in her studio, thinking, replaying the conversation over lunch. She was convinced Tommy Whitaker was a sly operator, a manipulator. But was he a killer? That, she didn't know. His explanation was plausible, was it not? She examined her feelings, trying to put her finger on why she felt such rage. She realised that the focus of her anger was Paul, not Whitaker. In a good marriage, you back up your partner, right or wrong, don't you? He had left her out to dry, made her look like a hysterical fool. At that moment she hated him. He could fuck right off if he thought he could disregard her feelings like that. She would stand up for herself. She was not going to let him take that contract.

Decision made, she looked at her watch. Two and a half hours before she had to pick up Davie and Jake from school. Time to finish the rabbit. She got her paints out, filled the jam jar and put the canvas on the easel. She stared at it. She knew she was not in the right mood to put the finishing touches to the delicate rabbit fur. She was in danger of destroying the light, whimsical feel of the piece in her current, dark mood. Instead she fetched a new canvas, tore off the cellophane wrapping and placed it on the easel. She made some quick slash-like pencil strokes, then reached for her paints, laying down layer after layer with confidence and assurance, building up and blending, using colour as she never had before. Two hours passed without her noticing. She was shocked when she looked at her watch. Oh Christ! The boys! It's nearly time! She laid down her brushes and took several steps back to regard the canvas from the doorway. The painting was semi-abstract, some areas left suggested, merging into the dark background, and some defined starkly with sure brushstrokes. The skin tone was extraordinary: she'd used greens and purples in unblended slabs to create the hollows and shadows, and it had worked. One eye was just hinted at. The other was painted in vivid detail, the scar a vicious slash of blue. The black background made the face leap out of the canvas with shocking effect. It was a horrible painting, ugly and menacing, but at the same time, the best thing she'd ever done. She'd painted Tommy Whitaker using all her emotion, and it had put her art on a completely different track, darker and more full of meaning. The rabbit painting propped up against the bookcase now looked like a child's effort in comparison. She was amazed at herself, and pleased. Well, something good has come out of today after all, she thought.

**

The boys were in high spirits as they tumbled out of the school gates. Jenny had just managed to get there on time. As she stood next to the other mums with their smart jackets and immaculate hair, she realised what a mess she herself looked. She was still wearing her paint-smeared jeans and her hands were covered in purple and black splodges. She'd probably got paint on her forehead; that always happened when she pushed her hair back. Oh well, never mind; the painting she'd done earlier had released her pent-up energy, and she felt calm and almost cheerful as she walked back towards the house. On impulse she called out to the boys, galloping on ahead:

'Jake, Davie! Want to play on the swings?'

'Yeah!' they shouted, and veered off towards the park.

Jenny sat on the bench and watched as they competed to go higher and higher on the swings. She forced herself to resist telling them to slow down. Her boys, the most important thing in her world. Just look at them flying through the air, so carefree and confident. She would have to be careful to shield them from any arguments with Paul. They worshipped their dad – a bit unfairly, she thought, considering how much more time she spent with them. Or maybe because of that. She made herself promise not to confront Paul until the boys were asleep.

'Come on. Time to go now,' she said, after a while.

The evening passed in a whir of normality. Homework and dinner and a bit of television before bedtime. She read a chapter of Harry Potter, and kissed them both before turning out the lights.

'Night, boys. Sleep tight.'

Then she poured herself a glass of wine and waited. And waited. Eight o'clock passed, then nine, then ten. Still no sign of Paul. He's avoiding me, she thought. Or else making a point. Eventually, she gave up and went to bed. She would tackle him in the morning.

Sleep came surprisingly quickly. She did not hear Paul come in, well after midnight, and slide guiltily into bed beside her. If she'd been awake she might have noticed that his breath smelt of beer; there was another smell, too, almost masked by the alcohol. Light and floral. Like soap. Or maybe perfume. But Jenny slept on deeply, unconcerned, as Paul reached for the alarm clock with a clumsy hand and put out his bedside light.

21

'We need to talk.'

'Not now, Jen, I'm done in.'

'Yes, now. I want to get things out in the open. You've been avoiding me.'

Two days had passed since that awful lunch. Paul had been getting home later than ever, and deliberately leaving the house early in the morning while she was still in full flow – making the breakfast, nagging the boys to get dressed, checking their school bags and wrapping up their packed lunches.

'Davie and Jake are in bed. I want us to have a calm conversation about what happened at that lunch. Please sit down, Paul.'

Paul heaved a sigh. His expression was hard to read. There was stubbornness, impatience, but also, she thought, a hint of wariness in his eyes as he sat down at the kitchen table. Jenny closed the door, then took the seat opposite him.

'I'm so mad at you. I asked you to come with me to back me up. To give me moral support. You didn't do that. You fawned all over that odious man instead.'

'Wait a minute, wait a minute. Let's get a few things straight first. Now, be honest, totally honest. Do you really still believe you saw him dump a body?'

'Honestly, I'm not sure. But yes, I think there's still a possibility that he did.'

'Right, a *possibility*.' His voice dripped with sarcasm. 'So you admit he might well be innocent. Of course he's bloody innocent! Any fool can see that! He's no more a killer than... than... your dad, or mine! In which case you have absolutely no reason to dislike the man.'

'He was condescending, sly, definitely sexist...'

'You're just pissed off he spent more time talking to me! That we had a bit of rapport.'

'Am I hell! He was ridiculous, false, the whole thing was a pretence aimed at putting me off the trail. There was no real rapport, he was reeling you in like a fish on a line.'

'Oh, listen to you, you selfish cow! You want the whole thing to be all about you, don't you? How you feel, what you think? You're jealous! You couldn't stand not being the important one.'

'Paul!' She was shocked, stunned, by the sudden outburst. 'This is me you're talking to! When have I ever been jealous of you? I'm trying to make you see sense! The man is not to be trusted!' She took a deep breath. 'You're not to take his business.'

'Now, you listen to me! No, just be quiet and listen for once,' he said, as she prepared to interrupt. His voice had a hard edge that she'd never heard before. 'I have been slaving at building my business for more than a year. I work so hard, such long hours. All you do is complain. You don't realise the struggle that it is – it's not just the security work, which is complicated enough, but all the other crap that goes with it– training up an employee, paying the bills, chasing up the invoices, prospecting for new clients, paying taxes, insurance – you don't have any idea, sitting upstairs in your little studio making cute little pictures of dogs and cats. You don't live in the real world.

'How would you survive on the money you bring in? You

wouldn't! Your art business isn't exactly thriving. This house, the cars, the holidays abroad – everything depends on me making a go of my business. And it's touch and go right now, let me tell you. We're only just breaking even. Did you know that? Have you ever even bothered to ask? No! You just give me that disappointed look and moan about me being late all the time.

'Tommy Whitaker is a multimillionaire with a decent hospitality empire. This contract would be worth a lot. It would put us in the clear for the next year, maybe two, at least. It's money, Jen, money, that dirty word. But money, sadly, is important.'

Jenny shook her head, trying desperately to find a better argument. 'You can't take his business. It's a ploy. If you worked for him, then I wouldn't be able to testify against him, for example, in court.'

Paul let out a snort of disbelief. 'Go to court? Go to court?' He gave a bark of laughter. 'What makes you think any court would listen to your story? Yes, Your Honour, we were ten years old, Your Honour, yes I'm sure, Your Honour. Get real!' Paul's voice was rising in pitch and Jenny glanced at the door, worried the boys would hear.

'Shh, calm down,' she hissed. 'You'll wake them.' She struggled to find a compromise, a middle ground. This conversation was not going how she planned. She was astonished by the depth of his resentment towards her. She tried to see his side of things. 'Listen, Paul, I know you work hard and I really do appreciate that. If I often sound tetchy, it's because I'm tired too. The boys can be hard work. I'm sorry your business isn't taking off as fast as you want, but it's such early days. It will grow, I'm sure. I believe in you. But please don't take his business. You can call it whatever you like, gut instinct, feminine intuition, but that man is bad news. It won't work out. Forget about the body in the lake – I think he's a charlatan and he will screw you over. Please don't touch it.'

Paul gave her a cold stare. 'Too late. I called him yesterday,' he said, flatly.

He stood up and left the room, leaving Jenny gaping after him in dismay. This is not us, she thought. We never have rows like this! How long has this resentment been building up? Have we been growing gradually apart without me noticing? And where does this leave our marriage?

22

'Hello, Dora. It's Jenny again. I was just wondering if there's any news about Claire? Any progress?'

Jenny had spent the last week in a haze of confusion. She and Paul were no longer speaking, although they made every effort to be normal when the boys were with them. Jenny swung from feeling aggrieved, hard-done-by and bitter, to nervous, tearful and unsure. Was it her fault? Was she self-obsessed, living in a comfortable bubble, while he carried all their financial responsibilities? But the next moment she would remember his cutting words, his disdainful comments about 'cute paintings' and 'middle-aged housewives' and her blood would boil again. Housewife! How fucking dare he! She was the one who made it possible for him to work all hours, by doing everything else in the house. And she did have a career, even if the money it brought in was a drop in the ocean compared to him; it was enough to pay some of the big bills - the insurance, the gas, telecom. That wasn't nothing. And she was still building a reputation, it takes time, time for word of mouth to kick in. She tried to talk to him, to open up some lines of communication so they could find their way back to each other, but he didn't seem to be interested. He had closed off, shut down. Tommy Whitaker was not mentioned, and she didn't dare ask whether or not he had signed a new contract.

She desperately needed something to take her mind off things, some good news. Maybe Dora would provide that.

'Sorry, dear, there's not much change, I'm afraid. They say she's no longer aggressive or self-harming.' Claire had apparently tried to smash her window, cutting herself in the process. 'But they don't think she's ready for the group sessions yet. The doctor said she's not receptive, whatever that means. He says she's still suffering from delusions and paranoia. He even asked me if there was any schizophrenia in the family.' Dora's voice trembled, and Jenny could tell she was crying. 'I don't know what to do! She's our little girl and she's suffering! It must be our fault. Isn't it always the parents' fault, the upbringing? We didn't make her strong enough to take all these terrible knocks she's had. And that... that awful husband of hers. I feel I could kill him, I really do!'

'You mustn't blame yourself! You were wonderful parents. Absolutely wonderful! I used to love staying at your house. And it's never just one thing that causes people to break; it's a combination. Everyone has a cracking point, and Claire just found hers. And actually, I don't think there's anything fundamentally wrong with her, mentally - she's just been really clobbered by events.'

'Thank you dear, I do hope you're right. And things are still ganging up on her. Poor dear. I can't believe it. It's one thing after another. The divorce, then finding out he had a new girlfriend so quickly. And then a baby, when they tried for so many years to have one. And now her flat.'

'What about her flat? What's happened?'

'Well, it was a bit scary. Ken and I went round to her flat, you see. We thought we'd better empty her fridge and take the post out of the letter box and that kind of thing, in case she has to stay in the hospital for much longer. It's what we did last time. Oh gosh, did you know she'd been in the hospital before?'

'Yes, she told me.'

'Oh, I see. I'm glad she told you. But when we got to her flat, the door was sort of open. Well it was closed, but we could just push it open. I think the lock had been forced, although we didn't see any damage. We went in and checked everything. It was a bit frightening; we didn't know if anybody was still inside. I made Ken go in ahead of me and check the bedroom and bathroom.'

'What did you find? Was anything stolen?'

'No, not much. It was all quite neat and tidy, really. But we couldn't find her laptop. She did have a laptop, didn't she? I'm sure she did. I think that must have been taken. It was strange though, they didn't take her handbag. Her purse was still inside.'

Jenny's thoughts swirled. She'd almost convinced herself that Claire's obsession with Whitaker was just that: an unfounded obsession. A conspiracy theory with a follower of just one. But now this. A break-in. Her laptop, with all her painstaking research into financial irregularities and missing persons, was now gone. Jenny felt a creeping sense of dread.

'That is strange,' she said. 'Did you report it?'

'Yes, we made a statement at the local police station. I think it's just for insurance purposes really. I don't think there's any chance of getting the laptop back. The police were very kind and sympathetic, but they said there have been a string of break-ins in that part of Manchester recently. Her flat is in quite a nice area, so I was surprised. But I suppose burglars go to the nicer areas, don't they? For better pickings. The policeman said they usually focus on high technology-type things that they can sell on quickly, like mobile phones, and, um, tablets and laptops – things that are hard to trace. They didn't seem too surprised about the handbag still being there. They said they usually go for jewellery too, which they pass on to people to melt down. But we checked Claire's jewellery box. Her wedding ring and engagement ring were still there. Anyway, we're off to the shops tomorrow to replace her laptop. Actually, Jenny, maybe you can help. Do you know a lot about computers? Can you recommend a good one?'

Jenny felt a little reassured to know there had been a spate of local burglaries. Maybe that was all this was. She promised to ask Paul for advice about what laptop to choose. They chatted for a further twenty minutes, Jenny trying to provide some comfort by talking about mundane things like the weather, her boys, her parents.

'Mum and Dad send their love,' she finished. 'They said if there's anything they can do to help, you must tell them.'

'I know. They phoned yesterday. So kind. But all we can do now is wait and pray, really. Goodbye dear. And thank you for phoning.'

'Bye Dora. You take care. Ken too.'

Jenny sat thinking for a long while after she put the phone down. She heard the boys upstairs, playing a noisy game when they should have been starting homework, but decided to ignore them. She didn't know what to believe. She took a notebook from the drawer and made two columns, one for her dark suspicions, and the other for their more logical explanations. Claire had thought she was being followed. Was that true? But then the doctor had identified paranoia as part of her condition. Did she jump in the canal? Try to end it all? She was definitely depressed, maybe suicidal. She'd just seen that heart-breaking baby photo. She had already attempted suicide, only a short time ago. But what if she was pushed? She told me to be careful, she was definitely scared. No, that was too far-fetched, surely. But now her laptop was missing. Was it a targeted break-in aimed at destroying the evidence she'd built up? Or just a random burglary by young vandals looking to convert anything they could grab into money for drugs? The two columns ended up being of equal length, leaving her no further forward. She needed a sounding board, someone to bounce her ideas off. That's what husbands are for, for God's sake, she thought, sourly. It's Paul I should be able to go to with all this. But that was impossible. She considered phoning DI Fielding again, and setting out all her theories, but decided against it. It had been too humiliating last time. Should she phone her dad? No, he would worry too much. Then an idea: I'll phone John in Orkney! She lifted the phone up once again and dialled, calmed by the idea of laying her worries at her big brother's door. He had been a scientist before his early retirement. He would be able to bring logic to bear. But there was no answer. The phone rang and rang, then cut to the answerphone. Not so surprising really, the mobile reception was always patchy up there, especially if he was out walking his dog. Jenny didn't leave a message. She wouldn't have known where to start.

She remained immobile in her seat as the thoughts whirled about, swinging first one way, then the other. She had no idea how long she had been sitting there, when she noticed movement in the doorway. She jerked back to the present with a start. Davie and Jake had appeared, looking a bit lost. Davie was holding his school bag.

'Mum, you haven't checked my homework diary,' said Davie. 'You always check it. Look, I got a gold star today. And I need you to help me revise my spellings.'

'Oh, sorry! I was miles away.' She gave them both a reassuring smile. The boys must come first, she admonished herself. 'Come on then, Davie, hop up here and let's have a look.' Davie leapt onto the sofa with her and opened up his bag.

'Jake, what about you? What homework have you got?' she asked her eldest.

'We didn't have any today. Mum...?' Jake looked cross and moody. Jenny knew that look. He was worried about something.

'What is it, darling?'

'Where's Dad?' he asked. 'When's he coming home? Will he be reading the story tonight?'

Oh no, thought Jenny. She realised with a sinking heart

that the boys had picked up on the tension in the house. They were on edge, aware that something was amiss. Usually so adept at juggling everything, she had let this particular ball crash to the floor. It wasn't fair on them and it was up to her to reassure them.

'Oh, sweetheart, don't worry. He's been working terribly hard this week, I know. Listen, I've got a good idea! Jake, fetch the coats. We'll pick up a McDonalds and surprise your Dad in the office. What do you say?'

'Yeah!' Jake was enthusiastic.

'But what about my homework?' worried Davie.

'Pop your homework back in the bag, Davie, we'll take it with us. We can do it with Dad. Now, who needs the loo before we go?'

***

It was a long time since Jenny had been to Paul's work, and despite the recent tension between them, she was excited to see the place again. Paul had rented office space in a shared business hub. The ultra-modern building consisted of three floors; the first floor contained a big open space for co-working, a second floor was split into glass-walled cubicles for private offices, and a third floor contained break-out spaces, kitchens and showers. There was even a gym in the basement. It was all very smart and professional, designed to impress clients, but the rents were surprisingly reasonable. It had been a good choice of location for a start-up business, as there was plenty of room to expand in the future. Paul's office was on the second floor, next to a chill-out area with state-of-the-art coffee machines, comfy chairs and a pool table. Jenny fished the card out of her bag and held it to the magnetic card reader, and the heavy glass door clicked open. She pushed it wide, and the boys shot though, leaving her to struggle behind them with the carrier bags full of food. As she knew they would, the boys galloped upstairs and went straight to the pool table, all thoughts of food forgotten, leaving Jenny to continue alone down the corridor. This was a peace offering. Not only would it cheer up the boys, it would signal to Paul that she was ready to make the first move. They would get over this!

She smiled as she made her way along the blue carpeted hallway towards Paul's glass box. Then she stopped. She froze for a long moment, then put the bags down on the floor. She looked up again, aware that her heart had started beating too fast. There was her handsome husband, at his desk, looking at his computer screen. And next to him, so close that their two heads were touching, was his new employee. Marianne. She too was looking at the screen. Both of them were smiling, complicit, engaged in the moment. Marianne's glossy dark hair swung prettily as she dipped her head to say something to Paul, and he laughed, easily. The two of them looked so comfortable together, so right, that Jenny suddenly felt as if she was receding backwards into the distance, shrinking, frozen out. She could not take her eyes away from the scene. So innocent on one level; they were not quite touching, nor were they exchanging passionate glances, but she knew, instinctively, that there was more to this scene than appeared on the surface.

Jenny remembered helping Paul choose his new employee, sifting through and second-reading the stack of applications from a woman's viewpoint. She could still visualise the photo that Marianne had included on the top left corner of her CV: serious, hair tied back severely, octagonal-framed glasses giving her an almost nerdy look. Twenty-eight years old with good qualifications and looking for a new challenge. Now, this same woman looked polished, beautiful and – what hurt the most – so young! So fresh and enthusiastic. This woman was obviously in love with her husband. And Paul? What was his involvement? The warmth of his look as he said something to Marianne broke her heart; how long was it since he'd looked at her that way? Could it be just shared joy over a successful piece of work? A technical problem solved, or a new client signed?

Then Paul glanced up and caught sight of her behind the glass wall. His reaction confirmed all her worst fears. He looked momentarily shocked, and pushed back with both hands against the desk to send his wheeled office chair shooting to the side. Then he rearranged his features into a welcoming smile, but not before Jenny had caught a fleeting expression of guilt. The moment was broken, as the boys pushed past her and barged into the office.

'Dad! We've got you a Big Mac!' Davie said, as Paul rose from his chair to hug them.

Jenny forced her expression into a cheerful smile and lifted the carrier bags high to show him.

'Fantastic! I'm starving!' said Paul. 'Let's go and eat in the chill-out room. Then I'll thrash you both at pool!' He put an arm round each boy and led them down the corridor, chatting and teasing them both in turn.

Paul the charmer, Paul the loving dad, thought Jenny bitterly. She stole another glance at Marianne, before following them. The young woman was staring after Paul and his children. She looked pale, her mouth slightly open. Then the two women's eyes met, and the younger woman dropped her gaze immediately, busying herself with the computer mouse. Her cheeks had reddened. Jenny felt almost sorry for her.

***

Jenny finally got the boys to bed. They were wildly overexcited after the high-carb meal and the many games of pool with their dad. But they were happy, reassured. Despite everything, it had been worth it to see their glowing faces. Jenny poured herself a big glass of wine and took the bottle with her to the living room. She tried to decide whether to confront Paul when he got in. She imagined what Claire's advice would be: don't make the mistake I made. Don't be too understanding, don't wait and hope. Yell, accuse and get it into the open. She geared herself up for the coming fight.

A short while later, she heard Paul's key in the Yale lock. She took another large gulp of wine and waited as he took off his coat and entered the room.

'That was fun, earlier,' he said, 'seeing the boys.'

Jenny stared at him, coolly.

'What?' Paul now looked annoyed.

'Sit down, Paul.'

'Oh God, what now?'

'Are you having an affair with Marianne?' There, she'd said it.

'Jesus! Of course not. Don't be ridiculous.' His defence was instant and convincing. No trace of the guilty expression of earlier.

'I saw the way you were together. I saw how she was looking at you. And I saw you shoot away from her when you realised I was there.' Jenny kept her voice calm and even.

'Christ sakes, Jen, you are so paranoid! What's got into you? Of course I'm not fucking having an affair. I haven't got fucking time to have an affair for one thing. Shit! I can't cope with this. I'm going up.'

'No, wait, talk to me!'

'I'm going to bed. I'll sleep in the spare room tonight.'

'No! The boys! They'll notice something's wrong!'

'Just tell them it's because you snore.' With a look which bordered on dislike, he left the room and walked upstairs, leaving Jenny staring after him.

Well, that went well, she thought.

23

DCI Hardcastle looked out of his office window with a troubled frown. There was DI Fielding again, scuttling across the car park. What the hell was she doing out there that couldn't be done inside? He watched as she took out her mobile phone and sat on the wall. Was she having personal problems? Hah! She looked such a dried up old stick, but what if she has a wild sex-life? he wondered. What if she's stalking a lover who jilted her, or setting up a swingers party. He chuckled delightedly at this idea, then stopped. There was another possibility. What if she was still chasing after Tommy? If she'd disregarded his orders? She wouldn't do that, would she? She wasn't the most ambitious officer, more of a plodder, slow and reliable. Not the type to go maverick surely? But he'd have to keep an eye on her.

He returned to his desk and busied himself once again with the budget review. Next on his daily list of tasks were the overtime authorisations to OK and the expenses sheets to doublecheck. A good day. He enjoyed getting to grips with the paperwork, where everything could be controlled and marshalled neatly into columns. He gave a satisfied grunt and uncapped his pen.

Then the phone rang. His mobile, not his desk phone.

'George? It's Tommy.'

'Tommy! What can I do for you?' Hardcastle kept his voice friendly, but suspected that his day was about to go downhill.

'We may have a little problem. It's your Inspector. The woman. Fielding, I believe her name is. She's been poking about, I'm sorry to say. She got in contact with the man who used to manage one of my old clubs, The Red Room, asking questions. Asking about missing girls, specifically. I thought you said you'd closed it down?'

'Damn. I did close it down. She's acting on her own, against orders. Did she get anything from him?'

'No, no. He came straight to me, of course. But I really can't have her talking to anyone else. You never know what people might say. What wild tales they might tell.' Whitaker's silky-smooth voice held a threat.

'Don't worry. I'll sort it.'

'You do that, George, old chap. You sort it out. Or else I will have to.' The friendly undertone was suddenly missing.

'What? Um... now look Tommy, don't worry, I'll take care of it this end.'

'Make sure you do. Just remember, George, we've had quite a connection over the years, haven't we? I'd *so* hate for people to... misconstrue our relationship.' He cut the call.

Fuck, fuck, thought Hardcastle as he put his mobile down on the desk. How the hell am I going to handle this? One mistake, back when he was a young DS. One bad decision, and he'd been caught, compromised. A few little tweaks, a few favours called in over the years, but nothing too bad. Nothing to make him feel he was a bad cop. His record was excellent. So many cases solved. So many villains put away. But now this! Tommy was clearly rattled. It wasn't the drug pushing that was worrying him, it seemed to be something about missing girls. What the hell had Whitaker done?

DCI Hardcastle was panicking. He'd had a long and successful career, passing his exams easily, learning to play politics, being promoted up the ranks. Just a few more years now and retirement beckoned with a healthy police pension. All that might now be in jeopardy. The pension, his reputation. Everything he'd worked so hard for. It wasn't fair. He gazed out of the window, the budget review completely forgotten. He had some big decisions to make.

24

The week had passed horribly slowly. Their relationship, which had been cool before, now turned frosty. Glacial. Paul had hardly addressed a word directly to her, instead communicating through the boys:

'Let's ask your mum to make some hot chocolate, shall we?' or 'Did your mum check your reading yet, or shall I do it?' and 'Do you want mum or me for the bedtime story?' It was infuriating.

Jenny threw herself into her work, starting three new commissions at the same time. She painted in the daylight hours, as usual, but as soon as the boys were in bed, she returned to her studio once more. She didn't want to wait downstairs, nervously, wondering when Paul would get home and what mood he would be in. Instead she worked, despite knowing that the harsh electric light would throw the colours out of kilter. She painted with a mad energy, swapping the canvases on the easel, working first on the shaggy head of a bull, then replacing it with the deep, trusting gaze of a golden retriever, and next with the sagging jowls of a bulldog. When she had the brush in her hand, she shut down all other thoughts and found some peace of mind.

She found it just about possible to maintain a normal, happy demeanour in the hours between the boys coming home from school and going to bed. But she was worried. The May half term holiday was fast approaching. Would she be able to keep up her cheery façade for a whole week without cracking? She allowed herself a good cry every day, once she'd delivered the boys to the school gates. It felt cathartic, necessary. She would no longer be able to afford that luxury in a week's time.

At least Claire seemed to be improving. The latest news from Dora and Ken was encouraging. They were being allowed to visit at last. Dora had been excited and nervous in equal measure when Jenny had phoned last night. She would phone them tonight to see how the reunion had gone.

As it turned out, she didn't have to wait that long. It was Claire who phoned her.

'Jenny, it's Claire!'

'Claire! Oh Claire! It's so good to hear your voice! I've been so worried!'

'I'm sorry, I couldn't contact you before now. I was so drugged up for the first weeks, I was completely out of it. Then they reduced the doses, but they still didn't let me use the phone. I've got the all-clear now to speak to people. Mum and Dad came here this afternoon. God, it was good to see them! They gave me a new mobile – my old one's at the bottom of the canal.' She gave a rueful laugh.

'But how are you? You sound so... normal! I mean, God, that sounds awful... I didn't mean....'

'I'm OK. Really OK. I'm fine. I just have to convince every-one here of that. I've got to play act for a few more weeks, give them what they want to hear. Then I should be out.'

'I'm so sorry about what happened. About the baby pic-ture and everything.'

'Yep, that was a nasty shock. I should have expected it, really. But that doesn't matter now. Jenny, listen to me and please try to believe me. Promise you'll try: I didn't jump. I was pushed.'

There was a long pause as Jenny assimilated this.

Strangely, there was no longer any doubt in her mind. She believed her.

'Tell me exactly what happened.'

'I was walking along the canal bank. Stupid idea, but I'd convinced myself I was being paranoid, and that I wasn't really being followed. There's a part of the canal where it gets really narrow and dark. I could hear someone behind me, a noise like a twig snapping or something. So I started to run, but I was grabbed from behind. Next thing I knew I was in the water, my head hurt, and I was sinking down. Then I woke up again. I was on the towpath, with all these paramedics around me. I tried to tell them in the ambulance and in the hospital that I'd been attacked, but I was completely incoherent. The knock on the head must have done something to my brain. I was talking, I knew in my head exactly what I wanted to say, but it kept coming out wrong. Total nonsense! I wanted to say 'Get me a telephone!' and it came out 'Get me a giraffe!' I tried to say 'I was attacked by a man' and the words came out 'I was in the van.' Oh God, it was so frustrating! And the more I tried to get through to the medics, the more rubbish my mouth was coming out with! It was almost hilarious. I was totally aware that I was talking rubbish, but couldn't help it. But it was so frightening too; I was panicking, thought I might have permanent brain damage and be stuck like that forever.

'Anyway, I ended up back at the psychiatric hospital – big surprise. And of course, they knew my history with the suicide attempt, and found out about Mike having a baby – I guess Mum must have told them. My brain was working again OK, but, of course, they didn't believe me for a minute when I said I was attacked. They put it down to denial, delusion, psychosis, all the rest. I tried and tried to explain the whole story to them – Tommy-bloody-Whitaker, the body in the lake – the more I talked, the more they were convinced I was off my rocker.

'I gave up in the end. I knew I'd never get out unless I

changed my story. So last week I started playing by their rules, admitting I'd been suicidal, going to sessions with the psychiatrist and talking about my anger issues, my grief at not having kids. It was easy to do, really, 'cos it's all kind of true. But I pretended to admit to the possibility that that the rest of it – the murder, being followed – was all in my head. I've been acting the model patient; doing the group sessions, making friends with other patients, eating my food, being a good girl. I even do art therapy! You'd be impressed! I needed to do everything right so they'd let me have a phone. So they'd let me talk to you. Because, Jenny, you could be in danger too.'

'God, do you think so? I'm not sure. Listen, Claire, a lot has happened here too. I think he tried to find another way to shut me up. I met Whitaker.'

'What? When?' Claire sounded panicky.

Jenny explained quickly about the meeting, and how violently she had disliked and distrusted the man. She described the driver of the black car.

'Did you get the number plate?' asked Claire.

'No, damn, I was too worked up. Shit, sorry. But it's got to be the same car, hasn't it? The same man who attacked you.'

She went on to describe Whitaker's explanation, and how Paul had been won over so easily by the man's oily charm.

'He said it was a curtain inside the carpet?'

'Yes. A gold silk curtain.'

'Did you believe him?'

'I didn't know what to think at the time. It sounded plausible. But now I'm sure. It was hair.'

'And what about Paul? What's he doing? Is he working with him?'

'I don't know. He said he'd phoned him. But we haven't spoken to each other for over a week. We had a huge row after that lunch. Really, oh God... really bitter. We said some awful things to each other. I think... I think the marriage is breaking up. I'm pretty sure he's having an affair with his colleague. A bit like you really,' she gave a short, ironic laugh. 'Younger woman. Newer model. Cliché, cliché.' The tears, always barely held at bay, started to fall again.

'Oh Jenny! Oh no! God, why are all men such pathetic arseholes? Jesus!' Claire was devastated for her friend. She knew what it was like to split up, knew the trauma that lay ahead.

'What do you think I should do?' asked Jenny. 'Do you really think I'm in danger?'

'You could be. I'm safe here in the hospital. He can't get me here. But you're exposed. You're on your own most of the day. I think you should get away for a bit. I'll phone that Fielding woman, I'm determined to convince her this time. I'll make her listen. But you should get out of your house. Did you know my flat was broken into? They took my laptop?'

'Yes. Your mum told me.'

'So you see, you're not safe in your house.'

'Oh God, the boys! What if someone breaks in when the boys are here?' An image flashed into Jenny's head of Davie coming down the stairs at night for a glass of milk and coming face-to-face with a man in a balaclava. 'I can't take that risk. You're right. I'm going to take them away. I'll go to John's. I won't wait for half term, I'll take them out of school early. Tomorrow.'

'Good. Good plan.'

'What about you, Claire? Are you sure you'll be OK?'

'Yep. I'm going to see this thing through to the end. I will not let them beat me.'

Jenny gave Claire John's address and phone number, plus Paul's mobile number, just in case. Then they said their goodbyes.

'Love you. Keep safe.'

'Love you, too. Be brave.'

25

'Right, boys! We're going on an adventure!' Jenny put on her most excited voice, clapping her hands and looking in turn from Jake to Davie. 'We're going to Scotland, to see your Uncle John!'

'Yay! Cool! Are we going for half-term?'

'No, even better! We're going today!'

'Today? But what about school? I've got a maths test on Tuesday,' said Davie.

'And there's the karate competition this weekend. I can't miss that. I might get a medal this time,' complained Jake.

'There'll be lots of other competitions. And lots of other maths test too, I expect! Come on boys, let's be a little bit naughty for once. Let's skip a couple of days of school and go to Orkney! Think of the beaches! The cool stuff we can visit before all the crowds turn up! Skara Brae! Maeshowe, the stone circle! We'll have them all to ourselves. It's going to be fantastic!'

Jake and Davie looked dazed. This was not like their mum. She never bent the rules.

'Is Dad coming too?' asked Jake.

Jenny hesitated, then decided on a little lie. 'He's going to join us later, if he gets all his work done. Now then, you two go and decide what games you want to take with you. It's a long old journey, so you'll need lots of stuff for the car. Can you remember where the Nintendo Switch is? You'll need that. Off you go!'

Please don't argue, please just go, she begged them silently, unsure just how long she could keep up the pretence if they dug their heels in. The boys looked bewildered, but both turned and headed upstairs to their bedroom, and Jenny let out a deep sigh. The cases were already packed and in the car. A triple room had been booked in an Inverness hotel for that night, and the ferry crossing reserved for the following day. The journey was going to be hell; a long drive with two tetchy, quarrelsome boys, but the thought of once more being in Orkney, with the wind in her hair and all worries left behind, was intoxicating. She realised how much she needed this break.

She took a piece of note paper and a pen, and sat down to write a note for Paul. He was going to be furious. Sod him, he'd forfeited the right to be mad. He could get stuffed. Clicking the pen open, she began to write:

I'm taking the boys away for a few days. We're going to Orkney to stay with John. I need a break. Also, Claire called. She says she was pushed into the canal and that I might be in danger. You won't believe that, but I think I do. If you want to put things right between us, you can come and join us. If you can spare the time off work, that is. Jenny.

She folded the note and put it in an envelope with his name on it, then cleared the living room table of all its junk and placed the envelope squarely in the middle. He would not be able to miss that.

She fetched their winter coats down from the cupboard in the hall, together with woolly hats and gloves; you could never quite tell what weather you were going to get up there. She stuffed them into a large shopping tote, put their walking boots in another, and took them to the car.

'You almost ready, boys?' she shouted up the stairs. 'Off in five minutes!'

She then went into the little playroom and pulled out the

box of storybook CDs, hoping they would keep the boys entertained for at least part of the time. She'd found them at a car boot sale, delighted with her discovery, but the boys had been less than impressed by the old-school technology, and they'd remained shut inside their box until now. But her car still had a CD player, and it was worth a try. What to choose... *Mr Stink*, of course. *Five children and It.* That should get them interested. And... ah yes! *The Famous Five Story Collection.* Two CDs, eight stories. That should keep them going. What could be more appropriate? It had all started with the Famous Five, after all. Two innocent little girls, looking for an adventure. She stuffed the CDs into her bag and ushered the boys outside, locking the door behind her.

She felt dizzy with relief as she started the engine and the house began to recede behind them. She was escaping it all: the fear, the confusion, the black looks from Paul – even the mundane chores of running a household. She was free!

***

Paul phoned her that night, as she'd expected. Jenny left the boys in the hotel room and went into the corridor, not wanting them to hear an argument. But Paul seemed more shocked than angry. Upset, shaken. Good, she thought. That'll teach him. It's about time he took me a bit more seriously. And it really won't do him any harm at all to look after the house for a week, cook for himself, iron his own bloody shirts, make his own bloody coffee.

'But why?' he kept asking. 'Why go now? Couldn't you talk to me first?'

'You haven't addressed a single word to me in about ten days. Why should I think you'd listen now?'

'But the boys, taking them out of school... it's a bit dramatic. We'll get fined.'

Jenny had actually laughed at that. 'That is honestly the last thing I'm worried about right now. Claire was pushed, Paul. Didn't you read that bit? Someone tried to kill her!'

'Yes, but...'

Jenny didn't let him finish. 'Don't try to tell me again she's a nutter, it's all in her head. It won't wash. I believe her. My life is in danger. And to be honest, getting away from you right now is going to do me a power of good.'

'But you can't just...'

'I've done it, Paul, there's no 'can't'. Get used to it. If you won't take the threat seriously, then I must. Claire's going to talk to that police inspector again. Hopefully things will get sorted, but I'm damned if I'm putting myself or the boys in harm's way, just because you can't see what a fucking crook that man is. He is a murderer, Paul. A murderer.'

She'd never talked to Paul this way before, with absolute conviction, with authority. He seemed stunned.

'OK,' he said, quietly, after a pause. 'Do what you have to do, Jen. Look after yourself and the boys. Drive carefully. Watch they don't run about like nutters on the ferry. I'll phone you tomorrow. And Jen?'

'Yeah?'

'Take care.'

Jenny went back into the room, a thoughtful expression on her face. That had sounded almost like the old Paul, the one who still loved her. Maybe there was still hope.

26

'Oh, God, it's so good to be here!' said Jenny, clinking bottles with John before taking a long pull from her beer.

They were sitting on the decking behind John's wooden chalet, wrapped up in warm coats and woolly hats against the chilly Orkney evening, watching the boys throw sticks for the dog in the field beyond.

Jenny smiled as she watched Jake and Davie run about madly, pushing each other over, fighting for the stick, laughing, and getting very muddy, as the dog barked and capered about around them. She felt a wave of relief; they had been cooped up in the car, bored and disorientated, for most of two days, and they needed to let off steam now. Surprisingly, they seemed to be getting on well; there hadn't been any of Jake's barbed jibes lately. Maybe the confusion of their rushed trip north had thrown them into realising they needed each other. The short ferry crossing had provided the only break from the car. They had stood together on the upper deck, filling their lungs with blasts of cold sea air, watching the gannets wheel upwards and then plunge like spears into the water. The boys had been entranced. Then it was back in the car for the last part of the drive to John's new home.

Jenny had visited only once before, but the weather had been grey, misty and miserable for the whole visit. Now, as she got out of the car, her breath was taken away by the beauty of the scene in the late afternoon sunlight. The modest chalet stood in an isolated spot. The only nearby building was a traditional stone farmhouse, fifty metres or so away, where John got his milk and eggs every day. Below both these buildings the freshwater loch was a sparkling blue. Tall reeds glowed golden in the sunshine as they danced in the ever-present breeze. Jenny recognised the loch from the photos of goldeneye, tufted ducks and the occasional Greenland goose that John sometimes posted on Facebook. And above the two buildings, a gentle sweep of pale green farmland gave way to the steep rise of the sea cliffs, where John would often climb to photograph the kittiwake, guillemots and, if he was lucky, the odd puffin.

He had greeted them on the doorstep, high-fiving the boys and giving Jenny a big hug. Jenny buried her face in his Icelandic sweater, then pulled back to look at her big brother. He looked well. He had been living on Orkney for two years now. The move had surprised everyone, and had dismayed their parents. John had been a well-renowned molecular biologist, living a semi-nomadic life as he travelled the world with each new job. He went from research institutes in the USA, to universities in Germany and medical facilities in Asia, his reputation growing with each move. But then, suddenly, he had given it all up to come to this isolated island. No-one thought it would last, especially after two hard winters, when the sun shone for barely six hours a day, and the storm winds made it impossible sometimes even to get his front door open. But as Jenny looked at him now, she could tell he was thriving. His long, sensitive face was more relaxed than she had ever seen it, and the wild weather had given him a deep tan. His eyes twinkled with amusements as he watched the boys struggle to pull their cases out of the boot. He was dressed in old cords, muddy boots and a thick sweater, and he looked completely at home.

'My God, look at you! You've gone native!' she cried. 'You look really happy!'

'I am. Life's good here. Simple.'

From inside the chalet there came a volley of frenzied barking, and Davie looked suddenly frightened. The boys hadn't met John's dog before.

'Don't worry about Loki,' John told them. 'He's really very friendly. But he's only six months old, and still a puppy really, so he gets very overexcited. He may jump up a bit, but just push him down and say 'no!' very firmly. I'm still training him.'

Both boys had been understandably nervous when the door was finally opened and the dog flew out. He was huge; part Husky, part Alsatian, with one eye that was brown, and the other a startling bright blue. With his thick black and cream-coloured fur, he looked much more wolf than dog. Davie had shot behind Jenny, his arms clinging to her waist, and even Jake had taken a couple of steps back. Gradually the fear was replaced by curiosity, and then excitement, as they realised they had a ready-made playmate with inexhaustible energy.

'Look at them go,' said Jenny now. 'They are loving it here! Thanks so much for having us. Sorry it was such short notice. I hope we haven't put you out.'

'No, no, of course not. I didn't have any plans. My days are all very similar; I get up, I walk the dog, I eat, I take some photos or I go fishing. I walk the dog again and I go to bed. It's a lonely life in a way, but it suits me fine. But just now and again, it's really nice to have some company. So this was a very nice surprise. It's great to see you all! But it was a bit unexpected. What was all the rush?'

'It's a long story,' said Jenny, finishing her beer. 'Get us another couple of these, and I'll fill you in.'

John returned with another two bottles and sat back down, stretching out his long legs in front of him. Jenny let out a breath, and started to explain.

'I've got myself in deep trouble. I'm running away, really.'

'What from?' John was amazed. This was out of character.

They were very different people; he considered his sister to be a conformist, lapping up the suburban lifestyle and enjoying all its material trappings. He himself had come to Orkney with not much more than a bed, two chairs and a record collection. How had his straight-and-narrow sister got into trouble?

'What are you running away from?' he asked again.

'Two things. From Paul; we're not getting on well. But also from danger. My life might be in danger.'

'Bloody hell! What's happened?'

'You remember Claire?'

'Yes, of course.'

'You remember she used to come and stay in the summer holidays or at half term?'

'Oh yes. I used to feel really jealous!'

'Jealous? Did you? Why?'

'You two used to be such a closed club. An exclusive little twosome. I was shut out. I lost my little sister when she came, and I used to really resent her for it.'

'Really? Is that why you used to be so nasty when she was there? Teasing us, making fun of our games, trying to steal our secret papers?'

'Yes, I suppose I was a bit of an arse. So what about Claire?'

'We used to play in that old house, the one you showed me, do you remember? Blackmere Hall, it's called. We used to steal in through the gap in the railings and poke about, looking for a mystery.'

'Oh yes, the famous Mystery Book! I read that. I remember thinking it was a load of crap. Go on.'

'Yes, well, we found our mystery, all right. One day, when we were hiding in the woods there, we saw a man dump the body of a woman in the lake.'

'Bloody hell!' exclaimed John again. He listened as she

told the whole story, leaving nothing out.

'I can't believe it!' said John when she'd finished. His expression was grave. 'My little goody-two-shoes sister mixed up with money laundering and murder! Shit!' He was quiet for a long moment, as he took in the news. Then he lifted his forgotten bottle to his mouth again, took a gulp of beer and said: 'Well, you can all stay here as long as you like. Don't go back until you know it's safe.'

'Thanks, John. So you think I did the right thing coming here?'

'Yes, I do. And I'll make sure you all have a good time, too. Make it a proper holiday for the boys. You can forget all the stress and just chill out. I'll take the boys fishing. We can visit all the archaeological sites. Are they into bones and Vikings and stuff?'

'Oh yes, the gorier the better!'

'Right. Tomorrow we'll start exploring. I'm sure they'd like the Tomb of the Eagles. You go into a stone age tomb one by one on a little trolley. And in the visitor's centre they let you handle five thousand-year-old bones, axe heads and pottery. It's family run; a normal museum wouldn't let you anywhere near stuff like that. Maybe they'll even let the boys touch a skull.'

'They will absolutely love that! Can we take the dog?'

'Yeah, Loki can come too. It's a good cliff walk up to the tomb. Good for seal spotting too.'

'Great.'

Jenny felt a huge weight lifted from her shoulders. She had an ally now, someone who believed her, and had her back. She would be perfectly safe here, she thought.

But she was wrong.

27

Paul put his key in the lock and pushed the door open. The emptiness hit him again in a fresh wave; no lights, no noisy children, no smells from the kitchen. No life at all. Jenny and the boys had been gone for five days now, and he didn't like it. The house seemed to blame him somehow; it was no longer his friend. The washing machine had broken down as if in protest, and he'd burnt a small hole in the ironing board. He'd forgotten to take the bins out, and now they were overflowing with the takeaway cartons he'd collected. The stack of empty beer cans in the kitchen was growing and the house had started to smell of alcohol. He began to feel sorry for himself. Then a flash of anger: she had deserted him! Left him to cope with everything and gone swanning off on holiday! He didn't deserve this! He wandered around the house aimlessly, looking for comfort. There was her letter, replaced in its envelope and perched against the fruit bowl. He didn't need to read it again; he could remember every word, especially the bitter jibe at the end. There were the boys' video games, abandoned in a messy pile on the floor. He should really tidy them up. Instead he went upstairs to the spare room, Jenny's studio. He stood for a long while, studying the three animal paintings that were leaning against the bookshelves. She's really pretty good, he thought, surprised. The animals were clearly recognizable from the photos that were Sellotaped to the top of each canvas, but at the same time, strangely abstract. Colours that shouldn't work seemed somehow to work well. The angles were brave, striking. She's got something, he thought. Then he noticed a fourth large canvas, turned to face the wall. He picked it up, turned it round, then placed it on the easel. He stepped back in shock, the impact almost physical. The eye that stared back at him was brimming with menace. Christ! Is that how she sees Tommy Whitaker? She must really hate him, he thought. But the likeness was unmistakeable. He turned the unsettling picture to face the wall again, and wandered into the bedroom. The bed was unmade and he pulled the duvet up roughly, to cover the pillows. On Jenny's side he saw her pile of books on the bedside table, her magnesium tablets, her collection of favourite earrings in a little bowl. For some reason these objects made him feel immeasurably sad. Get a grip, he thought. She hasn't died. She's on bloody holiday!

Back downstairs again he pulled out the take-away menus from the 'useful drawer' in the kitchen, but found he didn't really fancy anything. Instead he got another couple of cans of beer from the fridge, grabbed some peanuts, and went into the living room to watch TV.

It was well after midnight when Paul stirred in his sleep. Through the fog of alcohol, he thought he'd heard something. A clunk. The front door opening, or maybe closing. Was it Jenny, had she come back? Suddenly wide awake now, he listened intently. There was no noise. No boys climbing the stairs, no thump of cases in the hall. He'd been mistaken. Or maybe dreaming. The house was silent. He rolled over to Jenny's side of the bed, put his head on her pillow and thought he could catch a faint whiff of her scent.

He slept deeply once again.

28

'What's a groatie buckie, Uncle John?' asked Davie.

'It's a tiny little shell, no bigger than your little fingernail. It's white, or sometimes pinkish. And the legend says it brings you good fortune. Here, here's one I keep in my pocket for good luck.' He showed the boys the minuscule, porcelain-like shell with its delicate ridges and narrow opening along one side. 'It's like hunting for treasure. They're very difficult to find because they're so small. I bet you both a pound you can't find one today!'

Challenge accepted, the boys raced off ahead of them along the wide, sandy beach, pausing occasionally with eyes down and hands locked behind their backs, stooping to examine the shells and pebbles at their feet.

Jenny and John walked slowly behind them, listening to the rhythmic crashing of the waves onto the shore, followed by the gentle tinkling sound, as the waves pulled back again to the sea. Jenny was equally as absorbed by the hunt as the boys, all worries forgotten as she searched for the tiny shell. The wind whipped her hair into her eyes and she held it back with one hand.

Loki ran continually from the boys to the adults, uncertain who to protect, giving the occasional sharp bark to urge them to stay together.

The previous days had been a triumph. The boys had

adored lying face-up on a little wooden trolley and scooting backwards through a narrow, pitch-black tunnel to reach the stone age Tomb of the Eagles. They were awestruck to be allowed to handle the Neolithic axe heads and knives, but also just as excited to be eating tubs of the local ice cream, sitting on a bench outside the visitor centre, shivering with cold. John had a knack of telling the boys just enough to fire their imaginations, without lecturing them. They lapped up his stories of eagles picking human bones dry, Neolithic human sacrifices and Viking murder plots. They hadn't seen much of John during his working lifetime, and now Jenny could tell that he was fast becoming their favourite uncle.

'I've found one! I've found one!' shouted Jake, running back to them.

'Let me see?' John examined the shell. 'You have indeed! Well done! I owe you one pound. Your turn now, Davie.'

John linked an arm through Jenny's and gave it a squeeze. 'Feeling better?' he asked.

'Infinitely!' she replied with a smile. Her cheeks were flushed and her eyes bright. The dark circles had disappeared. John thought she looked a different creature from the wan, weary woman who had arrived at his door four days ago. He decided to broach a tricky subject.

'So what's going on with you and Paul? Should I be worried?'

'I don't really know. We seem to have grown apart without either of us noticing. He spends so much time at work. He's obsessed with his job, and I feel like he's been ignoring me and the boys.'

'But you always knew you'd married an ambitious man. You had to expect that a bit, didn't you?'

'Yes, I guess so. I don't mind the time he spends at work so much as... as... the way he seems to disrespect the things I do. He's not in the least interested in my work, and he takes the other stuff I do – the housework, the homework, all that stuff – completely for granted.'

'That's typical of a lot of men, isn't it? I know it shouldn't be that way these days, but...'

'Yeah, I suppose. But most women of my generation wouldn't stand for it. It's weird, I've been trying to work out where we've gone wrong. You know, when we got married we were equals. We both had our degrees, we both had projects and hopes for the future. I even had the better job when we first started working. A bigger salary. I knew he'd go places, but I thought his drive and determination would rub off on me and that he'd help me achieve amazing things too. But it's turned out that his career shot off into the stratosphere, while mine just sort of fizzled out. I'm not saying it's all his fault; it's mine too. I've settled for less. I've ended up more or less just being a housewife with a hobby. Oh shit, John, I've turned into our Mum! How the hell didn't I see that coming?'

John laughed. 'No, you're not quite there yet. At least you can drive! You don't have coffee mornings and watch daytime TV and get your hair set every week, do you?'

'Well, kind of! I'm in a book club! That's pretty much the modern equivalent of a coffee morning. Only with wine instead of coffee. Oh Christ, what have I been wasting my time with? You know, it was Paul who encouraged me to become an artist, he seemed to really believe in me. But now... it's ironic. The fact that I work from home means he expects me to do more household stuff. Fair enough, but it also means he has less respect for me. I'm making his life easier, and he knows that and likes that, but at the same time doesn't really appreciate it. And the way he speaks to me, well... sometimes he treats me as if I don't have a brain anymore.'

'Hmm. I can see that would drive you crazy. But your artwork is good. You shouldn't do yourself down. It's more than just a hobby. Hmm... I don't know... I think sometimes it's hard to break away from our parents' role models. We subconsciously seek to recreate the patterns they created, because they give us security. Maybe you *are* a bit influenced by Mum. She's an absolute sweetheart, but she's a typical middle class product of her generation. She never worked, and never really expected you to either. The height of her ambition for you was to marry a man who could support you! Even for me it was a struggle to break free of their expectations. Being a man, I was expected to work hard and marry. I know they can't understand me living here, alone, being retired. It's not following the mould and it makes them feel insecure. What about Paul's parents? What was their relationship like? Was his mother a stay-at-home mum?'

'Oh God, you couldn't ever call her that! She was chic and fierce and opinionated. But no, she never worked. She was a committee fiend. Went round terrifying everyone in the village.'

'And what does Paul think about the Blackmere Hall story? I gather he hasn't been supportive?'

'Worse than that. He doesn't believe me. He thinks Claire is crazy and made the story up, and that I've gone along with it because I'm gullible. You see, he doesn't really credit me for having a mind of my own any more. And... and... I think he might be having an affair.'

'Really? Oh no! You always seemed so good together. What makes you think so?'

'Just instinct, really. The way his assistant looks at him. The way he looks at her. The late nights. I might be misreading the signs, but I've got a really bad feeling. I think we're breaking up. I'm scared of what that'll do to the boys. They worship him.'

'Oh, Jen.' He gave her arm another squeeze, but offered no advice. They continued up the beach in step without further words. Up ahead they could see Davie waving excitedly. He'd found his shell.

'Anyway, enough about me. What about your love life?' she asked, as they were about to reach the boys. 'Why did you never get married?'

'I don't know. Never found the right guy, I suppose.'

'The right... oh! Oh John!' She stopped and faced him, mouth open in surprise. Then she threw her arms round him and gave him a tight hug.

'What a hopeless pair we are!'

29

'Stop being so pathetic and get the bloody hoover out!' Paul said to himself as he walked into the hallway. The house was definitely starting to smell of ancient take-aways and stale beer. He ran upstairs, threw off his work clothes and changed into a T-shirt and jeans. Catching sight of himself in the mirror, he thought he was beginning to look a bit rough. His thick sandy hair was uncombed and falling into his eyes. He had two days of pale stubble on his chin, and not in a macho, George Clooney-type way. His emerging beard was coming through a rather un-attractive ginger. Oh, for goodness sake, he thought. Your wife's been gone for less than a week and you're letting yourself go! He went downstairs and made a start on the kitchen, throwing all the tins into a black plastic bag and taking them, together with the cardboard food containers, down to the bins at the end of the street. Next he opened the downstairs windows and looked under the sink. Where did Jen keep the furniture polish, he wondered. What stuff does she use? The wood stuff or this other stuff? He squirted out a jet of each and decided the wood stuff smelt better. Whistling to himself, he wiped down the book-shelves, the TV stand and the window sills, then put the jumble of video games on the floor into a neat pile. I should do this more often, he thought. It's not so hard. Next, the coffee table. As he bent down to release a jet of polish, he did a double-take. Jen's letter.

He was sure he'd left it upright, leaning against the fruit

bowl. He remembered staring at it last night; he'd been sitting on the sofa, and the letter had been directly in front on him. He'd stared at his name, rather miserably, written in her sloping artist's hand, as he'd opened up another can of beer. Had he moved it? Knocked it over? It now lay face-down on the table. It was just the smallest thing, the tiniest detail, but he suddenly felt uncomfortable. He thought back to the previous night, when he'd woken up, convinced for a moment that he'd heard the front door being opened or closed. No, you're imagining things, he thought. You must have moved the letter. Still something niggled. What had Jenny said? Claire's flat had been broken into and her laptop taken. Had the same thing happened here? He ran upstairs to the studio – no phew! There was her laptop case lying on the floor next to her box of paints, exactly where she usually left it. It drove him crazy, the way she was careless with her things. On the floor where anyone could step on it. He was about to leave the room when he turned back to check again. He picked up the case and knew immediately that it was empty. Had Jenny taken the laptop with her? But if so, why leave the case here?

This is crazy, he said to himself. You're getting as paranoid as she is. Should he phone Jen? It was late and he wasn't sure he could take her accusations right now. What if he phoned Claire? He could find her number through Jen's parents. But what would he say? How could he admit that he was having doubts to this woman who he'd written off as a nutcase for so long?

No, you are being stupid, he decided finally. It's dark, the house is too quiet, you've been drinking too much these last few nights and you've lost your focus a bit. You're getting spooked for no reason. The letter is flat on the table because you knocked it over. Jen took her laptop with her, probably wrapped up in a sweater. Everything is fine. Tomorrow was going to be a busy day. They had a valuable tender to bid for, and still had to finalise the last technical solutions and pricings before the deadline was up. Marianne was expecting him to turn up early, with a clear head. Pull yourself together, finish the cleaning and get yourselfto bed. You need to be fresh in the morning.

30

Time went by quickly. Jenny could see Jake and Davie becoming more relaxed with each passing day, no longer asking about their dad, or worrying about missed school. Instead they stuck to John like two extra puppies as he chased them round the huge standing stones of the Ring of Brodgar, or led them through the stone age alleyways of Skara Brae. Both became obsessed with Vikings, spending their evenings making newspaper swords and cardboard axes. Their uncle willingly played the hapless monk who they fell upon, alternately capturing or putting to death in the most gruesome way. John tried his best to distract Jenny too, finding galleries and craft shops that he knew would interest her. I wonder if I could live here, she thought, as they'd entered a little gallery-cum-café in Kirkwall. If we do split up? Start painting landscapes, birds and seals? Sell to the cruise ship passengers? It would be good to have John around, a male presence for the boys. They would lead a good life here, full of outdoor activities, contact with nature. She could almost picture it.

But as much as the boys were flourishing here, she herself was becoming more and more on edge. The first few days had been a huge release, a wonderful escape, but now her thoughts kept returning to home. What was happening there? Why had Paul not rung lately? Was he with that woman? Sleeping with her? Please not in our bed! And what had happened when Claire talked to Detective Fielding? Had she got anywhere?

Was Whitaker still driving around in his fat car with his hired muscle?

She asked herself what she wanted from life. Did she want to go back to normal, have the life she led before? Was that even possible anymore? Everything was different now. Or did she want to make a totally fresh start, like John had done. Was she brave enough? But then, was it fair to uproot the boys from everything they knew; their school, their street, their house, their dad. That eternal question: do you put up with things that aren't perfect for the sake of your kids, or do you look after yourself first? Grab the life you deserve? Tell yourself that a happy mum makes for happy kids?

She'd spent the morning sitting in one of the saggy old armchairs John had bought from a charity shop, staring at the logs in the log-burner, trying to find some answers. The boys had gone fishing with John, hoping to catch some trout. Loki was lying in front of the stove, uncharacteristically quiet for a change. 'Good boy' she said now and again, just to have some company, and he'd open one blue eye and thump his tail once on the rug. She looked at her phone and thought about calling Claire, but there was no reception in the chalet. She'd have to put on her coat and walk to the fence around the cattle field. She found she was just too lethargic.

And then the boys burst in, and Loki leapt up, tail swinging madly from side to side. Jenny stood too, making a big effort to snap out of her gloom.

'Mum! Mum, look! We got five trout. Except they call them troot here.'

'Oh wow, they're beauties!' she enthused. 'We'll eat them for dinner tonight. Well done, you two!'

'Did you have a good morning?' asked John, following behind with an armful of fishing gear.

'Oh, I've just been sitting here like a lazy-bones all morning, eating sandwiches and watching the birds out of the window. I'm pretty sure I saw a short-eared owl though. Are you guys hungry?'

'No, we're fine. We packed a good old Scottish picnic. We've had scotch pies and sausage rolls and Irn Bru, haven't we, boys? Time for a cup of tea now, though.'

'Well, since you lot have all been so energetic, I think I'll take myself off for a walk too. What's the weather going to do, John, d'you think?'

'You should be OK for an hour or two maybe. There'll be rain later, though. Best go now, if you're going.'

Jenny fetched her coat and scarf and laced up her walking boots.

'Loki? You coming? Walkies?' But the dog just gave her an apologetic look and followed the boys into the kitchen, watching hopefully as they unpacked the picnic things.

Right then. Looks like it's just me, she thought, letting herself out of the house. Not even the dog wants me. She followed the road to the edge of the field, briefly distracted by the sight of the young bullocks charging from one end to the other. Then she struck off towards the cliff path. The wind was bracing, but it didn't clear her mind; her mood remained sombre. Everything's fucked up, she thought. My marriage, my home – everything I thought was so solid is slipping away. I'm not even sure I want to paint people's pets anymore. What's the point? What's the fucking point of anything? She pushed on blindly, her eyes streaming with tears, trying to avoid the heather roots and the mud. She was only vaguely conscious of the crash of waves against the cliffs and the tang of sea spray on her lips. The path became steeper and narrower. She skirted round the rocky inlets, boiling with sea foam, and stopped for a moment to catch her breath, looking out over the towering sea stacks, alive with screaming seabirds.

At last she was at the top. The path went no further, but stopped here at the highest point. The view was breath-taking.

White horses raced across the sea, and the clouds seemed to change every few minutes, first dark and angry, then sliver-lined as the sun broke through. The wind was fierce up here, and the hood of her jacket battered against her head with the strength of it. She took one step closer to the edge to admire the foam, frothing and bubbling below. The swell and fall was hypnotic. For one awful second she thought how easy it would be just to step off. All problems solved in an instant. Then a sudden gust of wind slammed into her back, forcing her to take a dangerous step forward and the spell was broken. God! What had she been thinking! She turned and hurried back to the wooden bench which stood several metres back from the edge. Here she sat for a long time, elbows on her knees and chin in her hands, gazing out to sea.

Gradually her thoughts took a new direction. She was healthy. She had two fantastic boys. She had friends and the best brother in the world. Wonderful, loving parents. She could paint. What the hell did she have to feel so miserable about? She had what so many people did not. She was probably stronger than she knew. It just hadn't been tested yet. She would have to find that strength and build the future that she deserved. And if that future was not with Paul, well, she would survive.

And as for Whitaker, that sad old bag of flesh with his ridiculous ginger hair and his Mr Toad suits – he could go fuck himself. He was not going to win. She would not let him. Claire would not let him. They would see him in hell!

The rain that John had predicted was starting to fall, and Jenny pushed her hood over her head and pulled the drawstrings tight. She'd spent too long up here. It was time to head back before the skies really opened. Damn, too late, the rain was suddenly coming across in horizontal sheets. She stood up and began to walk quickly towards the path. As she looked down, she was surprised to see a man several metres below, walking up the path. God, he's a tough nut, she thought, walking steadily in the rain with a bare head, eyes down, oblivious. He wore waterproof trousers, but his head was unprotected. The water must be going down his neck, poor guy! She formed her mouth into a sympathetic smile, but then froze. There was something about his head. She could only see the top, but the hair was cut really short, like a soldier's. His shoulders too, they were massive, muscly, under his jacket. She had seen that hair before. Those powerful arms, but last time they'd been barely contained inside a shiny black suit. Then the man looked up at her and smiled. It was not a pleasant smile. Just an upturning of the lips in that square face, the eyes remaining cold, calculating.

Jenny looked about wildly, searching for an escape. To her left the sea boomed and thundered as it crashed into the caves below. To her right the yellow gorse was thick and knotted, forming an impenetrable wall. And below her, a killer, climbing upwards with slow, steady footsteps, the smile still in place on his massive face.

31

Jenny backed away, searching desperately for an escape. The bench! She ran behind it, but knew that this would never hold him back. It would be farcical, like some 1920s silent comedy, each one running round, changing direction, anticipating. It would never work. He was metres away now, looking directly at her. She noticed his eyes for the first time. Pale blue, expressionless. There was no choice. She launched herself into the gorse.

So deceptive. Such beautiful, innocent, sunshine-yellow little flowers, hiding inch-long spikes as hard as wood. She had barely taken two steps before she was completely imprisoned; her jacket, her hair, her jeans, all pierced and held fast by the sharp needles. She struggled, but to no avail. She screamed as his hand shot out and gripped her arm. She heard the material of her jacket ripping and felt a stab of intense pain as strands of tangled hair were torn from her scalp. He swore and grunted as he pulled. Then suddenly she was free of the gorse, but now he held her in front of him in a vice-like grip. One arm was round her neck, the other round her waist. Both her arms were pinned against her body. She could smell his sweat. The rain was dripping from his head onto hers. He began to slowly back her towards the edge of the cliff.

She screamed again, but the wind took her voice away. She kicked out with both heels of her boots, aiming at his shins and kneecaps. It did not seem to have any effect. She could hear the crash of the waves getting closer and closer. Two metres.

One metre. She couldn't die like this!

Then, suddenly, she felt his grip release. One hand was still round her neck, but the other was lashing out at something behind him. Twisting her head, she saw that his leg was gripped between the jaws of a snarling wolf-dog. The waterproof trousers were torn and she could see blood on the dog's bottom jaw. The man was landing fierce blows on the dog's head, but still it did not relinquish its hold. Loki! Now they were two against one. She couldn't let him harm the dog! With her free hand she reached down and scrabbled blindly on the ground for some weapon. She felt pebbles, roots, grass. Then finally she had it. She curled her hand around a heavy, sharp rock and with a massive effort, twisted out of his grip, swinging the rock and smashing it with all the force she could muster against his head.

The man dropped instantly, swinging round as he fell and landing on his front, arms splayed. Loki sprang back but remained crouching, teeth bared, ready to attack again, but the man did not move. Jenny dropped to her knees and let the rock fall from her hand. She was panting, her heart was thumping in her chest. The dog glanced at her quickly, and gave a slight movement of his tail, before returning his gaze to the prone figure. All was still. Seconds passed as the rain continued to fall, streaming down Jenny's face.

Gradually, Jenny became aware of her name being called. Someone was hurrying up the cliff path. That brown jacket. She knew that jacket. But still her brain refused to make the connection.

'Jen! Jen, Jen! Are you OK?' Paul lifted her up and folded her into his arms. She remained stiff and unyielding, incapable of a response. Her mind was void.

'Are you injured? Did he hurt you?' Paul released her from his arms and looked at her, taking in her torn jacket and the trickle of blood running down from her hairline, turning pink as it mixed with the raindrops.

Jenny stared at him, uncomprehending. 'Paul?' she said, at last.

'Yes, it's me. Jen I'm so sorry. I'm so sorry!'

'What are you doing here?' she managed, in a whisper.

'I missed you. I was worried about you. Oh God! I thought he was going to push you over the edge! I didn't think we'd get to you in time. Oh, thank God, thank God you're OK!' He hugged her tightly once again, and this time Jenny put her arms around his back and buried her head in his jacket. They stood locked together for several minutes. Then Jenny pulled away.

'Did I kill him?' she asked, hardly daring to look at the body on the ground.

'I don't know. I'll check his pulse.'

Paul knelt down beside the prone figure, lifted one of the meaty hands and held his fingers to the wrist.

'I think there's a slight pulse. His leg is a mess and his head's pretty bad.'

'What are we going to do?'

'We do exactly what he tried to do to you. We throw him over the edge.' Pauls voice was firm, with no hint of uncertainty.

'What? No! We can't do that!' Jenny was astounded.

'Listen, Jen, he tried to kill you. He tried to kill Claire. We get rid of this piece of shit.'

'Jesus, Paul, no! What's come over you?'

'No-one does that to my wife. Come on, help me lift him. Grab his legs.' Paul had already taken hold of the man by the armpits.

'No! I won't do it. We'd be murderers, as bad as him. We'll go to the police.'

Paul stood up again and put his hands on her shoulders. He looked deep into her eyes. 'Jen,' he said, gently, 'I'm not sure that's such a great idea. What's it going to look like if the police come? His head's all bloody. He might be dead by the time they get here. There's only our word that he attacked you. They might charge you with his murder. Or me. Let's finish it now, cleanly, no fuss.'

'We could just say we found him like this, couldn't we?'

'What, and let him go unpunished if he's still alive? And what if the police wanted to have the dog put down? No. We chuck him over the edge. Come on.'

'No, I can't. I won't.'

Paul sighed and ran his hands through his wet hair, thinking hard. Jenny thought back to her first visit to a police station. She remembered the feelings of shame and frustration as she and Claire had laid out their story, only to be summarily dismissed. She wasn't sure she could bear another police interview, more questions, more suspicion. She knew going to the police was the correct thing to do, but all strength seemed to have deserted her.

'OK,' Paul said, at last. 'There's another solution. We leave him here. It looks like he's injured pretty badly. The weather's going to get very cold tonight, I guess it'll be only two or three degrees above freezing. And with this rain and the windchill, I don't think he'll make it through the night. He'll die of exposure. Let's just go. Leave him here. Leave it up to the elements to finish him off.'

Jenny was suddenly exhausted. She had no more fight left. Let Paul figure it out, she was done.

'OK,' she said.

'Hand us that rock, the one you hit him with.'

'What are you going to do with it?'

'I'll put it under his head. Then if anyone comes they'll think he was attacked by a dog, fell and hit his head on the rock. Accident.'

Jenny averted her eyes as Paul gripped the man's short hair, lifted his head and placed the blood-stained rock underneath. Then he turned back to her.

'Come on. Let's go.'

They made their way slowly and carefully back down the steep path, with Loki running on in front. Jenny looked back once. All she could see was a black lump. It could have been a rock. She shivered and looked at the ground again, concentrating on getting down safely without slipping.

***

'There you are! You look like a pair of drowned rats! Get into the warm, quick.' John held the door open. Then he noticed Jenny's torn jacket. 'Are you OK? What happened to your coat?'

They had agreed not to tell anyone what had happened on the cliff-top. Not John, not Claire. Paul had taken control of the situation, and Jenny had let him make the decisions. She felt incapable of rational thought. Her mind kept repeating 'I've killed a man, I've killed a man.'

'I fell in the gorse,' she said, now. 'If Paul hadn't come, I'd still be there. I didn't realise how deadly it is!'

'God, yeah, it's awful stuff. I've seen dead sheep in the gorse a few times. It traps you completely. You're lucky he was there! We'd have sent out a search party eventually, but you'd have been stuck for ages.'

John took in her pale face and wide eyes. She looked like death. She was shivering. Was it the shock of Paul turning up? Had they had words? He felt a surge of protectiveness. If this man was hurting his little sister, he'd... Then he stopped. Other people's marriages were a mystery, and it was best not to interfere. Let them sort it out for themselves, and be there to pick up the pieces.

'I'm going to run you a bath,' he said now. 'Paul, the whisky bottle's in the cupboard over the cooker, and glasses in that cupboard there. Pour us all a shot, will you?'

After the bath, Jenny felt a little better. She was about to pull the plug and release the water when John called from the corridor: 'Leave the water in. My idiot dog's been eating something disgusting again. Probably a dead rabbit. I'm going to stick him in the bath.'

Poor dog, she thought as she pulled on her pyjamas. What a reward for such heroism.

Half an hour later, John was in the tiny kitchen, cooking the trout. Fabulous odours were drifting into the living room, where Jenny and Paul sat together on the sofa. The boys were on the rug in front of them, playing with the dog's ears and stroking his wet fur backwards. Loki didn't seem to mind.

'Tell us again how you saved Mummy, Dad! How did you rescue her?'

Paul camped up the story, beating his chest like Tarzan as he mimed racing up the hill, wildly exaggerating the size of the thorns, mimicking her helpless cries of 'Help! Help', and puffing out his chest as he mimed pushing the gorse aside to reach her. The boys were entranced, and even Jenny smiled. They were a united family again, just for now.

That night, she could not sleep. Paul lay beside her, one arm still protectively round her body, but she could not relax. In her mind, she kept on repeating the gesture, the swing of her arm, the thud of the contact, the blood. She listened to the wind howling around the cabin. She heard the rain hammering against the windows and imagined it hitting the body, high up on the exposed cliff top. He would be dead.

I killed a man, I killed a man, she thought.

32

John was first up. He made a pot of tea and poured out two mugs. Then he tapped gently on the bedroom door.

'Jenny? Paul? Are you decent?'

'Yes, come in!'

'I've brought you some tea. Listen, I thought you two might like to have a day by yourselves today.' John put the mugs on the bedside table, then paused in the doorway. 'You've probably got stuff to talk about without the boys hanging round. I thought I'd take them out for the day. We'll do Maeshowe in the morning. I think they'll like the Viking graffiti there. Then I'll take them for fish and chips in Stromness and they can buy a couple of souvenirs for their schoolfriends afterwards. How does that sound?'

'John, you are an angel. Sounds great. Shall I get the boys up?'

'I'll do it. You just have a lazy morning. We'll see you later this afternoon. I've been to the farm for eggs and there's bacon in the fridge, so feel free to make a fry up.'

With that he closed the door. They could hear the door of the tiny box-room next-door being opened, and John saying firmly 'Get down, Loki!', then giggles. Jenny guessed the dog had jumped on one of the beds. She had a sudden flashback to bared teeth and a bloody jaw. What an amazing animal, she thought, capable of telling friend from foe. She would spoil the dog rotten today. She hoped there was enough bacon.

Paul pushed himself up against the headboard and reached for his tea. He took a sip, then asked:

'How are you feeling today?'

'Not great. I didn't get much sleep. I kept thinking about… you know…'

'Yep. I know.'

'He must be dead. I killed him.'

'Yes, maybe. But it was self-defence. He very nearly killed you. You can't have any regrets, surely? It was the right thing to do.'

'But should we have left him there?'

'Yes. Absolutely.'

'What if… what if they find something of mine up there. Some of my hair in the gorse bushes? A bit of my jacket material?'

'They won't. I expect some walkers will find him. They'll see his leg, they'll know he was mauled by a dog, and they'll conclude that he fell. Don't worry.'

'I didn't know I was capable of… of what I did. I think I did it to protect the dog. I couldn't bear it that he was hitting Loki.'

'Idiot! Caring more about the dog than yourself. Well, I'm proud of you. Listen, do you want to us to walk up the cliff path again this morning and check that he's still there?'

'No! No, absolutely not. I suppose we should, but I just can't… Actually, no, it's a bad idea. If anyone saw us, they'd connect us to the body. Let's leave things as they are.'

'OK. Try not to think about it anymore. You drink your tea. I'll start the breakfast.'

He got out of bed, just wearing his underpants and Jenny was struck by his beauty. The definition of his jawline, the curve of his buttocks. He looked almost boyish, as he pulled on his jeans and his too-long hair flopped over his eyes. She was sur-prised to feel a rare stab of desire.

They ate breakfast together in companionable silence, then washed up side by side in the tiny kitchen.

'Come on. Let's take another cuppa onto the decking and talk,' said Paul. 'There's something I need to say to you.'

Jenny's heart stopped. She didn't know what to think of this. Was it a confession? An apology? Or was he going to say he was leaving her? He cared about her, that much was obvious. But was that enough? Did he still love her? Or was he in love with Marianne? She couldn't bear the anticipation, so when they were settled on the wooden chairs outside, she asked the first question.

'How did you get here? Why did you come?'

'Well, I suppose it started when I found your laptop was missing. I thought you might have taken it with you, but I just wasn't sure. Maybe someone took it. Then I just started to think 'what if?' What if you *had* seen a murder? What if Claire *had* been pushed? What if you were in danger? I had a ton of things to do at work, but I couldn't stop thinking about you, wondering if you were OK. So I got an early morning flight to London, changed at Aberdeen, then flew to Kirkwall, hired a car... When I got here, it was getting late. John said you'd gone up the hill for a walk. I wanted to speak to you alone, so I came up the hill after you. John said 'take the dog, he needs a walk', and he seemed willing enough to come along too. Thank God! Thank God he came! I would not have got to you in time. I would have seen him push you, watched you fall. It doesn't bear thinking about!'

'So you believe me now? About Whitaker?'

'Of course I do. Listen, I've been practicing what I wanted to say to you. There's some things you need to hear.'

'I'm not sure I can take much more, Paul.' She shut her eyes, scared of what was coming next. Oh God, oh God. You're leaving. You're leaving me, aren't you? she thought.

'Wait. Just listen. Jenny, I've been an idiot. I've been blind. I started to believe my own publicity. Started to think I was this superior intellect, the hotshot businessman. And at some point I stopped listening to you. I was so wound up in my own little bubble, I forgot that you were there too, coping, making it all possible for me. And worse than that, I started to treat you like the... sort of... little wife at home. I didn't really listen to you. I'm so sorry!'

'It's not all your fault. I didn't ask you enough about your work. I didn't understand it and I didn't try to. I was happy to have the easy life you gave us. We ended up living in two different worlds.'

'Yes, we were sort of moving in parallel, without touching. Going down the same track, but at different speeds. And when you came to me with the body-in-the-lake story, I just wrote it off, thought it was just something you made up because you were bored and needed a story. I didn't take it seriously. And I nearly lost you! Christ! Can you forgive me?'

'That depends.' She hardly dared ask the next bit. 'Tell me about Marianne.'

Paul took a deep breath. 'OK. I want to be completely honest with you. I was tempted. I'm so sorry. We work really well together and share a lot of jokes at work. Things at home were, well, we were always sniping at each other. So, yes, we went out for a beer a couple of times after work, when I should have come home to you and the boys. That was wrong. I knew she wanted more. It wasn't fair to her either. But I was flattered. She's so much younger. She's pretty...'

Jenny flinched here. A memory came back: that glossy dark hair swinging as Marianne bent her head to Paul's. The two of them sharing a joke. Yes she was pretty. And so young...

'But she's just a kid,' he said. 'I didn't encourage her. Please believe me.'

'But you were tempted?'

'Yes. I suppose I was, for an instant. But nothing happened. I swear.'

'Being tempted is just as bad as if something happened. In your head, you wanted to sleep with her.'

'It was my ego. My massive, stupid ego. I promise nothing happened, and nothing will ever happen.'

Jenny looked sceptical. His description of the closeness he'd felt with Marianne really hurt. Hurt maybe more than any sexual misdeeds. He had wanted another woman more than he wanted her. Paul knew he had to do more.

'Look, I'll do whatever I have to, to make it better again with us. I'll get rid of Marianne. We can move. I'll even… I'll even change jobs. We can move to Scotland, closer to Dad and John. Whatever it takes.'

'It just takes time, I think. That's all. Give me time.'

'OK. I can do that.'

'And, well, there's more. If we're going to stay together, we need to change the way we deal with each other. We've got to talk more.'

'OK.'

They were silent for a long moment, watching a group of lapwing sweeping over the loch. Jenny felt tired, empty. But she had one more question.

'Did you sign a contract with Whitaker?'

'No, I didn't. He phoned twice, wanted to fix a meeting. I kept putting him off. I wasn't even sure why. I guess what you said about him screwing me over had made an impact. So I made excuses, said I was snowed under and we could meet later in the month.'

'Good.'

'So what now? How do we go forward?' he asked. 'Do you

want to go home, see Claire, go to the police again?'

Jenny thought. She wasn't ready for that yet. 'No, you're here now and the boys are having so much fun. We'll stay another three days, as we'd planned. Can you do that? Or do you need to get back to work?'

'I can do that. This is more important than work. You and I will talk to each other. See if we can work things out here, where it's peaceful. Then we'll go back.'

***

They spent the afternoon quietly, looking at the different birds through binoculars and trying to identify them in John's bird books. When the boys got home, they put on a united front, exclaiming over the souvenirs they had found.

'What on earth is this?' asked Paul, holding up the mug depicting a road sign that said Twatt.

'There's a real village called Twatt in Orkney! That's so cool! Twatt!' Jake's eyes gleamed as he repeated the word he wasn't normally allowed to use.

'Who's it for? I hope it's not for me!'

'It's for Grandad. And we've got a Twatt tea towel for Granny! And we found the real road sign and Uncle John took some pictures of us standing next to it! It's brilliant here!'

They had a pleasant evening, playing quizzes they found in John's extensive quiz book collection, secure and cosy in the log cabin, with the wood burner blazing and the dog pushing his nose into their hands in turn for attention.

But that night, after they'd put the boys to bed, Jenny's thoughts were again all over the place. Could she forgive Paul for being tempted? Did she want her old life back?

And would she really get away with killing that man?

33

When the police arrived at the house, Jenny was almost expecting it. She saw the patrol car pull up outside and the two men get out. One in uniform, younger, the other older, in plain clothes.

That's it, she thought. They've found the body. They've found evidence to put me at the scene. Or somebody saw me go up the cliff. I'll be arrested. They'll take me away from the boys. It was almost a relief when they knocked on the door. The dog barked a noisy warning, and John shut him into a bedroom before going to the front door.

As John showed the two men into the living room, Paul gripped her hand, whispering 'Be brave!' to her. She was trembling, all colour had left her face. The small room felt overcrowded, and suddenly much too hot.

'Come on, boys,' said John, tactfully. 'Let's take a bunch of cameras down to the loch. See what we can see.'

The boys were reluctant to leave, enthralled and curious to see real policemen at close quarters, but finally John persuaded them to go.

'Mr and Mrs Kerr?' said the older man in his beautiful, soft Orcadian accent. 'My name is Detective Inspector Tulloch. This is Constable Irvine. Would you like to sit down?'

Jenny collapsed onto the sofa as if her legs had suddenly lost all feeing. Paul sat down slowly beside her and grasped her hand. He looked questioningly up at the older man as he perched on the edge of the saggy armchair. The younger officer remained standing. He looked impossibly young, the acne still visible on his face.

'We've been contacted by the West Yorkshire Police Authority,' the older officer began, taking a notebook out of his pocket. 'They are looking for a man named Frank Marshall. He is wanted for the attempted murder of Claire Hastings – your friend, I believe?'

'Yes! Yes!' The dread receded and Jenny was suddenly elated. Claire had made a breakthrough. 'She was hit on the head and pushed into a canal!'

'Is that so? Well now, our West Yorkshire colleagues traced this man to Scrabster, where we believe he boarded a ferry to Orkney as a foot passenger. We believe he's on the island now. We've got a full description. We're trying to trace his movements. We think he hired a car under a false name. We've lost him, unfortunately, but we will find him. It's a small island and everyone knows everyone. A stranger will be easy to spot. In the meantime, we think you should take extra care, Mrs Kerr. You could be in danger.'

'OK,' said Jenny, cautiously. They don't know! she was thinking. He's lying dead on the cliff above their heads and they don't know! I'm in the clear! 'What should I do?'

'We would advise you to stay close to the house and don't go anywhere alone for a few days – at least, not until we apprehend him. We'll make sure to send a patrol car over here every couple of hours to check if everything is OK. Here's the number to call if you see anything suspicious, anything at all, or if you just need to talk to someone.'

He handed over a card, and as he did so, the springs of the old chair gave an audible squeak, setting off a renewed volley of loud barks from the bedroom.

'It sounds to me like you have a good watchdog in the house,' said DI Tulloch. 'Sounds like he's a big one too. You keep that dog close by, d'you hear?'

'We will. Thank you. We'll be careful,' said Paul.

Paul escorted the two officers to the door, leaving Jenny sitting on the sofa, lost in thought. Claire must have got through to them. There was a real investigation. At last! They would find out about Whitaker. And when they eventually found the body on the clifftop, well, they would identify him as a wanted criminal. Things were going to be OK!

Then the boys burst into the room, followed by John. He mouthed a silent 'OK?' at Jenny, and she gave a slight nod.

'Why were the police here, Mum?' asked Jake. 'What did they want?'

'Well,' God, what to say? There was no real danger now. The man was dead. The boys would need an explanation, but nothing to scare them too much. She improvised. 'There's a bad man on the island that they're looking for. He's been robbing some houses. They just told us to be careful, to lock the doors, and not to leave our windows open. Nothing to worry about too much. But we'll stay all together, just to be sure. I don't want you two going off on your own, even if you have Loki with you. OK?'

'OK, Mum.'

***

That afternoon, Jenny put on her coat and said: 'I'm just going to the fence to call Claire!'

'No, mum, the baddie might be out there!'

'Don't worry, Davie, darling, it's only a few metres from the house, and you can see me from the window. I'll take Loki with me.'

As she walked across the garden and approached the back fence and the field beyond, her mobile phone gave a series of dings. Messages. She pulled it out of her pocket and saw three messages and several missed calls from Claire. She felt bad: she should have called earlier, but she hadn't felt strong enough to lie convincingly. Now, after the police visit, she was optimistic. Everything was going to be OK.

Claire picked up immediately.

'Thank God!' she said. 'I've been so worried about you! That man, the driver, Marshall - the police say he's on the island! Are you safe?'

'Don't worry, Claire, I am completely safe here. I've got John, and Paul, and a very, very fierce dog to guard me. The police are searching for him. And a patrol car comes round here all the time to check. Nothing can happen. He can't get to me.' She felt bad about the lie; Paul still insisted it was better to keep things just between the two of them. The fewer people who knew she'd smashed a rock into Marshall's head, the better. Once everything was over, when Whitaker was arrested and the police enquiry closed, she'd tell Claire the whole story.

'What's been happening your end, Claire? Tell me everything! How did you manage to get the police involved?'

'Well, it was actually quite easy in the end. I was so surprised. It turned out that DI Fielding – she wasn't as bad as we thought. She'd been chasing things up. About the missing girls. She came to see me in hospital and took another statement. I got the impression the whole thing has taken off. She couldn't give me any details, but I think there's a real investigation now.'

'So is Whitaker still just carrying on as normal? Not arrested or anything?'

'I don't know. I don't think so, not yet.'

'Where are you now, Claire? Are you home?'

'I'm still at the hospital. It's safer here. But also...' she paused. 'It's actually doing me some good, I think. I've got a good new therapist, and we mainly talk about the marriage break-up. I've been finding out a lot of things about myself. I understand more about my reactions to things. It's really helping.'

'That's brilliant!'

'And, well, at first I just wrote off the other patients here as loonies. I couldn't bear to be lumped into the same category as them. But everyone's got a story, everyone is normal, really. I've actually made some pretty good friends. There's a woman with anorexia, and a guy with burnout... Or maybe I'm just getting institutionalised! It's safe here and people look after you. I'm not in such a hurry to get out anymore.'

'Great. That's sensible. You should stay there as long as you need to.'

'You said Paul was up there with you? Is he... are you two working things out?'

'Kind of. I'm not sure yet. He says he didn't have an affair, but, I don't know. He was definitely tempted. He's been grovelling, trying to make it up to me, but I'm not sure if I can get over that.'

'Yes, you can. If I've learnt anything here, it's that people are human. We all make mistakes. The important thing is to keep talking.'

'Wow! I thought you said all men were dicks! That I shouldn't take any shit! You've changed your tune!'

'I have, haven't I? Must be growing up at last! So is he staying up there with you?

'Yes, for the rest of the holiday. He's going a bit mental 'cos there's no Wi-Fi here. He's trying to do business on his phone and the signal's really bad. You have to come outside to get a connection. The boys love it here though. They have never had so much fun.'

'Good. Gosh, what's the time? I've got to go in a minute,' said Claire. 'Group session. Jenny, you take care! Don't take any chances! It'll all be over soon!'

'I will. You too! Love you.'

'Love you too.'

Jenny returned to the little wooden chalet with a smile on her face. Claire had sounded great! Positive, energised, happy. Maybe things would work out fine between her and Paul, too. The killing? She could probably put that behind her, rationalise it, in time. Everything was going to be OK.

That's what she thought...

34

Jenny had slept well, for the first time in a long while. She woke up feeling fresh and relaxed. She turned over in bed and looked at Paul's naked body. She knew it so well. The little blonde hairs on his arms, the whorl of sandy hair at the top of his head which looked like a mini tornado had landed on it. He looked so innocent, lying next to her, breathing deeply. The sex had been good last night. Slow, tender and giving. In the past, Paul had usually taken control, confident in his ability to satisfy her. But last night he had been uncharacteristically unsure of himself, which had made the whole act more equal, more intimate.

She pulled on her pyjamas and got up. She looked at her watch and saw it was not yet seven in the morning, but she felt wide awake. She needed a strong cup of tea to start the day. She wandered into the little galley kitchen and opened the fridge. Damn, they were out of milk. The boys had had cereals for supper last night. She put her coat on over her pyjamas, laced up her walking boots, and found a couple of pound coins in her bag. Loki wasn't around; she guessed he was sleeping in with the boys. She didn't want to wake them by calling the dog, so instead, she set off alone towards the farm.

It was a misty morning. She could only just see the outline of the farm buildings through the grey fog. The bottoms of her pyjama trousers were getting wet as she waded through the thick grass. The sun would burn off the mist later, and it was going to be a glorious day when it finally broke through. She pushed open the barn door and entered the gloomy interior. She walked past the milking stalls, taking in the rich aroma of cow dung. She'd always quite liked that smell. At the far end of the barn, she found the big fridge. She popped a couple of coins in the honesty box beside it, then took two bottles out. Lovely, creamy, fresh milk, virtually straight from the cow. Behind her, she heard the barn door bang. She didn't worry. Must be the wind, she thought. When is it ever *not* windy on this island! She turned round, a bottle in each hand.

The blow sent her flying. The bottles slipped out of her hands and crashed onto the swept concrete floor, sending a shower of glass and milk in every direction. She landed badly, hitting her head painfully against the edge of a cattle stall. For a moment she was stunned. Uncomprehending. Then she looked up.

She saw the cold pale blue eyes. The ugly gash on his temple. It was him. Marshall. Just for a second, she was euphoric; I didn't kill him! He's alive! But just for a moment. Then she realised the danger she was in. Even if she screamed, no-one would hear her inside this cold, empty barn. She put up two hands to protect herself as he approached.

'No, listen, don't hurt me! The police know. They know everything! They're outside!'

He laughed, without humour. 'No, they're not.'

'Don't hurt me! It's too late! They know about you.'

'We've got unfinished business, you and I. You thought you'd won, didn't you? Well, sorry, but I'm going to finish the job I came here to do.'

'No! No! Don't do it for Whitaker. It's too late! He's going to be arrested.'

'Oh, I don't think so. He'll be in Switzerland by now, I expect. You and me are going to find a nice, high cliff somewhere.'

She struggled to get up, but he was faster. He grabbed her

hands viciously and tied them behind her back. Then he flipped her over as if she weighed nothing at all and stuffed something in her mouth. She gagged as she tasted the foul material. As he dragged her upright and pulled her towards the door, she could hear his feet crunching over the broken glass. She was dimly aware that he was limping quite badly.

Outside, the mist was just as thick. She tried to scream but the noise that came out of her mouth was a muffled little moan. He crouched, then lifted her easily onto his shoulder, pinning her legs with one arm. Fireman's lift, she thought, bizarrely. Then he walked steadily towards the lane. She jerked her body, trying to unbalance him, but it was no use. His steps did not falter. She heard a clunk. A car door opening. Another click. He'd popped the boot. Oh, Jesus, no! He's going to put me in the boot. Again she tried to scream. He threw her roughly into the tiny space. She saw him reach one hand up to slam the boot down.

'Step away! Now!' A high-pitched voice, young, unsure.

Marshall swung round, and Jenny could finally see the figure behind him. It was the young officer, the one who looked barely out of his teens. Oh Christ, she thought, he doesn't stand a chance! He looked terrified and took a few steps back as Marshall swung a fist towards him. But then the young officer did two things. With one hand he put a whistle to his lips and blew a long, shrill note. At once Jenny heard a loud barking coming from inside the cabin. Simultaneously, with the other, he raised a canister and let fly a stream of spray, straight into Marshall's eyes. The big man cursed and clawed at his face with his hands, then stumbled away from the car towards the young constable. From her place in the boot, Jenny could no longer see anything. What's happening, what's happening? she worried. Is that poor young lad OK? But then the barking grew louder and she realised the cabin door must have opened. She heard shouts, scuffling, grunting and swearing. Then, finally, two hands reached into the boot and the filthy rag was gently removed from Jenny's mouth.

She gulped in the fresh air thankfully. Then she looked up at her husband. He was stark naked.

'You've got no clothes on,' she said, idiotically.

'I know. It's bloody freezing!' He lifted her carefully out of the boot, set her on her feet and turned her to face the car so he could start to untie the knot that bound her hands. 'Are you hurt?'

'A bit. Hit my head again.'

At last she was free. She turned and looked down at Marshall. He was lying face-down in the grass and the young officer had snapped handcuffs into place behind his back. The dog was letting out a steady, low growl as it positioned itself between the man on the ground and its master.

The officer unclipped his radio, fumbling and almost dropping it in his hurry, and started to call for help. Marshall struggled to a sitting position, then awkwardly tried to regain his feet. He stopped, swearing, as the dog sprang forward, teeth bared, and barked a warning.

'What shall we do with him now?' John asked the officer.

The young man seemed at a loss. He looked around, hopefully, mouth gaping, searching for inspiration. 'I don't rightly know, um... The boss will be here in about ten minutes...um...'

John took control. 'I'll get a rope to tie his feet. We'll carry him in and lock him in the small bedroom. It's not got a window, so he can't escape.'

As the men struggled to lift the heavy body and carry it awkwardly towards the house, two small boys watched in awe from the doorway.

'Did Daddy catch the bad man?' asked Davie.

'Yes. Daddy and Uncle John and the policeman. And Loki, of course. We did it together.' Jenny hugged the boys hard.

It was over. Finally.

35

DI Fielding could hardly bear to watch as DCI Hardcastle walked through the open plan office with a cardboard box in his arms. Her colleagues kept their heads studiously down, too embarrassed to make eye contact. He was suspended, pending an internal affairs investigation. The charge was 'accepting bribes in exchange for not reporting organized drug or prostitution rings or other illegal activities'.

Fielding was surprised. She knew some level of corruption was present in the force, but usually it was hushed up. The top brass brushed it away, or asked someone quietly to resign for health reasons, arguing that public trust in policing was more important than getting a conviction. But Hardcastle had pre-empted all that. He had come clean, admitted everything. He'd been taking bribes from Tommy Whitaker since the nineteen-eighties, in exchange for a degree of protection, advance warning of a raid, a blind eye here or there.

She had been dumbfounded when he'd done a complete about-face around ten days ago, briefing the entire team and pulling out all the stops to get information on Tommy Whitaker's drug dealing and money laundering. He'd also specifically asked Fielding to look into the missing girls, giving her the OK to bring whoever she wanted in for questioning. The team had worked hard, collating information from HM Customs, the National Crime Agency as well as interviews on the street, to build up a picture of Whitaker's empire. As Hardcastle encouraged and goaded them on, she'd realised what a good cop he could be. He seemed driven, tireless. She had developed a reluctant admiration for him, never suspecting that he had been on the take.

Now here he was, a sad figure, trying to open the door while awkwardly balancing the box on his beer belly. She felt sorry for him. On impulse, she left her seat and rushed over to hold the door. He gave her a pathetically grateful smile, and she decided to accompany him down the stairs and out into the car park.

He struggled again to put the box in the boot of his car, then turned to look at her.

'You didn't have to come down with me. But thanks. I appreciate it.'

'I'm sad to see you go, Guv. We've worked together for a long time.'

'I'm sad to be going. I can't pretend otherwise. It was because of you, you know,' he said.

'Sorry, Guv? What was because of me?'

'Why I blew the whistle on myself. I couldn't let him do anything to you. Whitaker. He threatened to 'take care of you'. I thought he might try to have you killed.'

'What, really?' She was shocked.

'That was the turning point, if you like. It was my red line. I couldn't let him do anything to you. You must believe me; I never knew he was … I only knew about…I honestly never knew about the girls. I would never have…'

'Guv, of course. You don't have to explain. And thank you. Thank you for not throwing me under a bus to protect your own career.'

'You're a good cop. You deserved better. Anyway, I'm getting old. About time I quit. I'll have more time for golf. Ha, ha.'

He attempted a smile, but it did not reach his eyes. Fielding laid a hand on his arm and gave it a slight squeeze.

'You take care of yourself, Guv,' she said, then turned and crossed the car park.

Hardcastle stared after her. He watched her push open the door of the police station and disappear inside. The finality of that moment, as the door swung closed behind her, made him catch his breath. He found his eyes were stinging with tears. He would so miss the buzz, the camaraderie, even the slow slog of police work.

'Well, you made your bed...' he muttered to himself as he lowered himself into his car.

36

It was just like last time, but then again it was totally different. Claire stood in front of Jenny's front door once more, a little nervously, and pressed the bell. She took in the well-planted front garden and the mature trees as she heard footsteps approaching. Paul opened the door, as he had last time, looking impossibly handsome and relaxed in a royal blue jumper and jeans.

But that's where the similarity ended. Last time he had stared at her, then stalked back down the corridor without a word, the stiffness of his back registering his disapproval. But this time he threw open the door, stepped out and enveloped her in a warm hug.

'Claire!' he said. 'I owe you the most massive apology. You must think I'm a complete bastard.'

'No, no,' she managed, rigid with embarrassment.

'Come in! Jenny's in the kitchen baking biscuits for some reason. Come on through. I'll put the kettle on.'

It was a Tuesday morning. The sun filled the kitchen with light, and Claire admired the black kitchen units against the stark white walls. Unlike the last time she'd been here, the kitchen was a mess. Drawing paper, felt tips and action figures were strewn over the table and the island was covered in flour. Jenny stood behind it, wearing a 'PRICK WITH A FORK' joke apron, her hands sticky.

'Hi, Claire! It's so good to see you!' Jenny rushed round and gave Claire an awkward hug, keeping her hands well away from the beautiful sage green jacket. 'I'm making shortbread. I think it's my self defence mechanism when I'm nervous – I bake!'

'Well, it smells great!' said Claire, taking off her jacket and throwing it over a chair. She was wearing a pretty red short-sleeved shirt and jeans.

Jenny noticed the change immediately. Claire's cheeks had filled out. She looked younger. Her arms, which had previously looked as if the flesh was barely covering the bone, were now rounded and pink. Her bottom, too, in the tight-fitting jeans, had a lovely curve.

'You look bloody marvellous! Really well!'

'I am well. I've never felt better, actually.'

'When did you get out? God, that sounds like you were in prison. Sorry! You know what I mean.'

Claire laughed. 'Got out is about right! Um, only recently. About a week ago. But it's all going well, so far.'

Paul shoved some children's drawings aside and put the teapot on the table, then went back for mugs and a milk bottle. As he squeezed past Jenny, Claire noticed how he gently brushed one hand along the small of her back. Aha! She thought. That's how things are!

'What time's she coming?' asked Claire.

'She said about ten o'clock. She should be here soon. I've been on pins. I couldn't sleep last night. How about you?'

'I feel OK, I think. Just really, really curious.'

The three of them chatted about safe topics for a while; about the boys' school, about Claire's flat and their summer plans, until they heard the doorbell ring.

'Oh shit, that's her! Crap, the biscuits!' Jenny tore off her apron and ran to the eye-level oven.

'Slow down!' said Paul. 'You two go and open up. I'll make

more tea in half an hour or so, and bring the biscuits in. Go!' He pushed Jenny gently towards the hall.

DI Fielding was out of uniform. She looked completely different, softer, younger, in rather old-fashioned corduroy trousers, a matching pullover and flat brown shoes. Much less intimidating. They ushered her through into the living room, and all took a seat.

After minimal pleasantries, Fielding got straight to the point.

'Right then. I wanted to come and give you both an update. First of all, Tommy Whitaker is in custody. We apprehended him some days ago, trying to board a flight to Zurich. Bail has been refused and we're interrogating him, although he is not cooperating. We have searched all his business and domestic premises and recovered some incriminating evidence. We're building a very strong case against him.

'Frank Marshall, the man who attacked you both, has agreed to cooperate. He has been giving us information in exchange for a lighter sentence. He'll be charged with two counts of aggravated assault, rather than attempted murder.' Here she looked at Claire and Jenny in turn. 'You may think this is too lenient, but our priority was to bring Whitaker to justice. I hope you agree?'

They glanced at each other questioningly, then both nodded.

'Tommy Whitaker will be charged shortly with drug trafficking, prostitution-related offences, gambling offences, tax evasion, and two counts of murder. The first murder relates to the body you saw being thrown into the lake. We have recovered and identified the body through dental records. It belonged to a young Irish girl named Mary Byrne. She was eighteen years old and worked as a prostitute in Leeds. The second murder took place nine years ago and was witnessed by Mr Marshall. It was he who later disposed of the body, and that body has also been recovered. Again it relates to a prostitute, this time twenty years old. We believe Whitaker was additionally responsible for the murder of at least three other young women, probably more. We are still in the process of investigating these, and they have not been added to the charge sheet, as yet. We have also been looking into historical complaints of sexual assault against him, and since the press got hold of the case, new accusations are starting to come in. We are investigating all these. So you see, it may take some time to completely conclude our investigation.'

'Why did he kill the girls?' Claire leaned forward in her seat, her hands clasped and her gaze intent.

Fielding looked uncomfortable for the first time. She was much more at ease talking about facts and figures. The psychology of murder was abhorrent to her and she found it more difficult to explain. She reached into her bag and took out a sheaf of notes. If she used the police psychologist's words, it would give her some degree of distance. She put on a pair of reading glasses and looked over the top of them to Jenny and Claire.

'This doesn't make very pleasant reading, I'm afraid. Some of these details are very distressing. Are you sure you want me to go on?'

Jenny hesitated, but Claire gave a firm 'Yes.'

Fielding looked down at her notes and began to read.

'This is from the police psychologist's report. *'Whitaker displays psychopathic behaviours; that is, a complete lack of ability to feel empathy or remorse for his actions. He can be further classified as a sexual sadist. That is, someone who can only reach sexual gratification from the suffering of others. This could be emotional or physical suffering, or both. In Whitaker's case, we can assume he is excited by physical suffering, coupled with a notion of domination and complete control. He sees himself as the ultimate predator and needs to induce terror in his victims in order to achieve climax. He would be capable of causing extensive, permanent, and potentially fatal suffering to achieve the necessary level of sexual excitement, regardless of the consent of the other person. Typical methods may involve beating, cigarette burns, mutilation, asphyxiation or strangulation. In day-to-day life, the psychopathic sexual sadist can present as charming and charismatic, making his activities difficult to detect. He may often keep trophies of his victims, such as underwear or films he has made of his acts. The degree of sadism generally increases over time. It is useful to talk to early girlfriends and partners to establish whether some form of sadistic sexual practices or fantasies were engaged in at that time. Typically, a sexual sadist will reach the climax of his activities at around fifty years of age, after which time such activities seem to stop. If detained by the police, the sexual sadist will appear calm and in control. He may talk freely, for many hours, giving little away. He considers himself to be of superior intellect. He will seek to manipulate the police questioning, and will be extremely interested to follow the outcome of the investigation. Two possible styles of questioning may be beneficial; if the interviewer is a younger female detective, his guard will be down and he may let something slip. He has a general disregard for young women's intelligence. However, if an older male detective takes the lead in the questioning, he may start playing mind games, again potentially revealing more than he intended.'* There.' Fielding looked at them over the top of her reading glasses. 'He is a nasty, nasty piece of work.'

'Oh, God, that poor young girl we saw!' Claire was almost in tears. 'She had no idea what she was going into. And she was so young, so pretty. Did she... Do you know what he did to her?'

'The decomposition was far too advanced to tell. Body decomposition is slightly slower in water than in air, but the length of time involved meant that most of the bones had detached from the skeleton. There were no breaks or knife marks on these bones, but it's impossible to say what flesh wounds there might have been. Two teeth were missing in the skull, which is rare in a girl that young. It could well be the result of a blow. You'll be interested to know that we found some remains of carpet material, as you said.

'In the second case of murder, which dates from the year twenty-eleven, we have a witness account from Marshall. And we have recovered a decomposed but complete skeleton. That girl had been beaten, mutilated and finally strangled.

'We believe Whitaker also abused other young girls with like-minded men. He invited these men to his clubs and filmed them in certain acts, later using the films for blackmail, extortion or influence.'

Fielding put the papers back in her bag and nodded slowly. 'We would not have known any of this if you both had not come forward that day. Thank you. You've helped us to put away a monster.'

'Will we have to testify?' asked Jenny.

'Not in the Whitaker case. But yes, in the Marshall assault cases, yes, you will be called to testify. We might be able to arrange to do this by live video link, if it's emotionally painful for you.'

There was a silence.

'Do either of you have any questions?' asked Fielding, standing up.

'No, I don't think so,' said Jenny. She glanced at Claire, who was staring into the distance. She looked ashen again, the healthy glow completely gone.

Paul had been hovering outside the door. He came into the room now with a laden tray, but Fielding didn't want to sit down again.

'I'm sorry, I can't stay any longer. But I did want to fill you in. You've still got my cards, so please phone if you want any more information. And I'll let you know as soon as I can, if we get a hearing date for Marshall.'

Jenny showed her to the door, thanking her once again for coming. When she entered the living room again, she was surprised to see Claire still in her seat, but with her knees pulled up and her arms crossed protectively around her body. Tears were pouring down her face. Paul was standing awkwardly behind her, handing her tissues. He looked over the top of her head towards Jenny, pulled a helpless face and lifted his shoulders, as if to say: 'Don't look at me! I didn't do anything!'

'Claire, what is it?'

'I don't know,' she sobbed. 'It's just... I feel so overwhelmed by it. That poor girl. All those girls. What men are capable of. What kind of world do we live in, where people like that can get away with things for so many years. There must have been so many cover-ups. Corruption. It happens all over. Take Jimmy Saville – he abused kids for six decades. Six! And Harvey Weinstein, he abused women for over thirty years. Now there's Jeffrey Epstein - God knows how long he was allowed to get away with raping young girls. It's men using women, using kids, men abusing their power. Again and again. Nobody lifts a finger to stop them. If you've got the money and the influence you can do what the hell you like. Even murder. I don't want to live in a world like that. I can't stand it.'

'Hey, come on, those men are the rare exceptions. Most people are kind and normal. Don't let it get to you!'

Claire blew her nose and made an effort to regain her self-control.

'Oh, you're right, I suppose. Don't mind me,' she said. 'I'm just being oversensitive.' She attempted a smile, but she was still shaking. 'I think it's coming off the antidepressants. I get overemotional. I don't think my reactions are quite back to normal yet. I probably just need to talk all this through, get a bit of help to process it. But don't worry. I'll be fine.'

'Look, we've both had a shock. We've had a glimpse into the underside of life. But life can be good, too. There's friendship, love, adventures, travel... lots to be positive about. Stay for lunch, please! We'll go out to a pub. Stay all afternoon! Meet the boys! We'll make this day a good day after all.'

'No. Thanks, but no. I'm going to go now.' She stood up. 'I'll just get my coat.'

Jenny followed her into the kitchen. She noticed that Claire's hands were still shaking slightly, as she lifted her leather jacket off the chair. 'Are you sure you're OK? You don't look so good. Maybe you shouldn't drive for a while. Stay a bit longer!'

But Claire walked quickly to the door. She hugged Jenny tightly, said 'Bye', then almost ran to her car. After staring after her for a moment, Jenny closed the door and returned to the living room.

'I'm worried,' she said to Paul. 'She looked just like she did the first time she came here. Really shaky. God, I hope she's going to be OK!'

EPILOGUE

They found a space easily in the half-empty car park. Jenny got out and opened the back door to retrieve her warm black coat. It was an unusually cold day for June. The sky was gloomy and rain threatened. Paul stepped out of the passenger side, beeped the lock and came to join her, giving her an encouraging smile, and together they made their way up the hill, past the pretty landscaped gardens with their circular rose beds and discreetly placed benches, to the modern brick crematorium. Jenny's black boots scrunched on the gravelled path noisily, breaking the silence. Paul gripped her hand.

'OK?' he asked.

'Yes, I'm OK. It's just… really sad. There doesn't seem to be anybody else here.'

'Well, we're a bit early,' he said. 'Maybe more will turn up soon.'

They waited under a leafy young tree, looking at the dozens of wreaths and tributes left along the paved pathway. There was something unbearably sad about the messages. 'To Dad' written in a child's hand, or 'Sleep peacefully, my love' in a shaky older hand. They watched as participants filed out of the crematorium from the service before; a mixed group of middle-aged and elderly figures dressed in black, walking in silence until they reached the gardens, then splitting into clusters to chat and reminisce. Jenny was shocked by the lack of pause between services. One in, one out. Next. Like a production line.

Still no-one appeared. Jenny glanced at her watch. People should be here by now! She couldn't bear it if the turnout was low. She looked down at the car park, but there were no new vehicles. Instead she saw the mourners from the previous service, getting into their cars, waving and driving away steadily, until just two cars remained.

As if to echo her mood, the sky darkened and a few spots of rain started to fall, leaving round grey splodges on the paving stones and making the flowers quiver. The ink on one card was starting to run.

Then, finally, two cars appeared. The first was a large black hearse, sombre and discrete. Two pallbearers in black sat in the front. Behind them, a simple pale brown coffin with one circular wreath of white lilies sitting on the top. The hearse pulled up outside the door of the crematorium, and the two men walked around to the back, extracting the coffin with ease and carrying it into the crematorium as if it weighed nothing. The second car had pulled up a short distance behind. Three elderly figures emerged, one woman, bent and walking painfully with a stick, and two barely more sprightly men. It was hard to read their expressions from their downcast eyes.

'We'd better go in now,' said Paul.

Jenny looked round again, hoping desperately for more mourners, but they were alone. She followed Paul into the building. The interior was stark. Grey, exposed brickwork lined the walls and austere wooden benches were arranged in a slight V-shape either side of the aisle. The three elderly mourners were sitting in the front row, heads bowed.

'Where do you want to sit?' whispered Paul.

'At the front, on the right,' said Jenny. She couldn't bear to think they were so few. If they went right to the front, it would create more atmosphere.

As they walked down the aisle, Jenny looked at the coffin, placed high on a marble block, with the single wreath now resting against the foot. A large photo stood on a stand beside it. A young, smiling face, shining with hope and optimism. Piped music filled the space as Jenny and Paul took their seats. Oh, no, not Ave Maria. She hated that mawkish, sentimental song. It did not fit with the vibrant young face in the photo. The celebrant took his place behind the lectern and welcomed the small gathering. Vaguely, she became aware of a door opening at the back of the room and another person, or people, entering and taking their seats behind. Thank God, she thought.

The service was shockingly brief and impersonal. The celebrant did his best to describe the life he was summing up, but he clearly had little idea who the person in the coffin really was. Maybe he had not taken the time to find out. Maybe he was too embarrassed to talk about the nature of her death. Instead he filled in with religious platitudes. She was now 'resting in peace' and 'with Jesus in Heaven.' And, worst of all: 'God moves in mysterious ways. We cannot know his will.' How can any God permit someone to die like that? screamed Jenny, silently. 'No God would ever permit that!'

Then, finally, they saw the curtains close over the marble block. Jenny imagined the coffin beginning its journey to the ovens. She shivered. The celebrant invited them to remain seated until close relatives had left, and once again they watched the three elderly figures make painful progress down the central aisle.

Jenny looked behind her. And smiled in grateful relief. At last! There was Claire, beautiful as ever in a long dark green coat. Her hair was caught up in a clip and she was wearing pair of green drop earrings which showed off her delicate neck. And beside her, a man, a stranger. She rose to join them, and together the four of them went out into the gardens.

'Claire! I didn't know if you were going to make it!' Jenny

said in a whisper, conscious of the surroundings.

'We almost missed it. I couldn't find the crematorium. I hadn't realised it was so far out of town. But I'm so glad we got here in time. This is Bob.' She grabbed the arm of her companion and pulled him into their circle. He was a tall, lanky man with a slight stoop. His tortoiseshell glasses and brown cord jacket gave him a rather bookish look. He smiled shyly and shook their hands. They talked for a moment about the service.

'Come with me to the loo, Claire?' asked Jenny, pulling her friend away and leaving the two men awkwardly looking after them, trying to find a mutually acceptable topic of conversation.

'Who's Bob?' asked Jenny, as soon as they were out of earshot. She was dying to know more. 'He looks nice!'

'He is nice. He's lovely. He's the one with burnout I told you about. The one I met in the hospital. We really hit it off.'

'That is fantastic! I'm so pleased!'

'Well, it's early days, but... I think he might be one for the long haul.'

'Oh, Claire! Wonderful! What does he do?'

'He used to be a magazine editor, a motorbike magazine, but you know, then he had burnout... He quit. He's going to retrain as a carpenter. He's got an apprenticeship, can you believe it? He'll be training with a load of teenagers. But it's what he wants to do, to work with his hands.'

'Is he single?'

'Divorced, like me. But amicably, unlike me. And do you want to know the best thing? He's got young kids. I get to play wicked stepmother. Or wicked step-girlfriend, at least. I'm trying not to get too fond of his kids, in case it doesn't work out, but it's hard. They are adorable. Anyway, what about you and Paul? Have you sorted everything out?'

'Yes, I think so. It's been pretty good actually. We're kind of rediscovering each other. We've talked and talked until we're sick of talking, but it's cleared the air. We know what we both need now. I've told him I want to go all out with my art and he's been really encouraging. He wants us to move to a house with an outbuilding so he can make me a proper studio, and he's been designing me this really cool new website. He looks after the boys when I've got a big job on. And I'm helping him with his work a bit too. I'm doing the books. So, yes, we do end up sharing a lot more, which is good.'

'What about the girl at his office? What was her name? Did she go?'

'Marianne? No, she's still there. The thing is, she's good at her job and he needs her. I'm a bit wary of that, but I've got to learn to trust him. It's coming. I think we're going to be OK.'

They hugged and turned to re-join the men who were walking back towards the car park. Then they stopped, suddenly aware of a small, black-clad figure shuffling towards them, her back bent and her trembling hand grasping a stick. When the old woman reached them, she looked up. She was tiny. Her deeply wrinkled face was full of character. Her mouth had fallen in where several teeth were missing, but her small brown eyes were sharp and alive. She smiled at them, displaying the gaps.

'You're them two girls, aren't you?' she said in a thick Irish accent. 'You're them two what's discovered my Mary. God bless you, dearies, God bless your souls. Now my Mary's at peace. It's taken so long. We've been searching for years and years. I never gave up, you see, but I was so scared I was going to die before we found her. Now I can rest, too. Bless you. God love you both.'

She picked up one of Claire's hands in both of her own trembling hands, and pressed it to her toothless mouth to bestow a papery kiss. Then she did the same with Jenny's. The dignity and emotion of the gesture was incredibly moving. Then the old woman turned and hobbled away.

Claire looked at Jenny with a kind of awe. There were tears in her eyes. Tears of happiness.

'We did it,' she said, her voice grave. 'We did that!'

The two women linked arms and walked down the gravel path, past the floral tributes, past the benches, past the rose bushes, and down to the car park, which was again filling up with cars, ready for the next service.

Jenny let out a sudden whoop of laughter, causing heads to turn in disapproval. 'Yes, we did,' she said. 'We bloody well did!'

AFTERWORD

If you enjoyed this novel, I would be so grateful if you could put a review on Amazon, or on Goodreads.
Thank you so much!

ACKNOWLEDGEMENT

First of all, enormous thanks to my excellent proof-readers:
-    Chris Sykes, for happily undertaking the tedious job of correcting punctuation, spelling and typos, for pointing out several anachronisms and for keeping me up to date about women's expectations of equality in today's world.
-    Cathy Shahani, for suggesting various ways to develop the characters and expand the plot.
-    Annie Leonard, for advice on the psychology of depression, therapy and psychopathy.

Thanks also to Carolyn Charlton, my childhood friend, former mystery detector, co-author and colourer-in of the original Mystery Book.

Thanks to my patient husband Gordon, who supported the writing process with equanimity, although he still hasn't read either of my books.

And finally, thanks to Alex, my irreplaceable friend, without whose encouragement I would never have written a book, and whom I miss every day.

ABOUT THE AUTHOR

Kate Leonard

Kate Leonard was born and raised in Wake-
field, West Yorkshire. She studied lan-
guages at Surrey University and worked
first as a tour operator, then later as a Ger-
man and French teacher. She has lived in
Switzerland, Edinburgh and Manchester.
In 1996 she moved to France with her husband, Gordon, and their two children. She
now lives in Grenoble in the French Alps.

PRAISE FOR AUTHOR

For Fall Line:
"One of those stories which captivates your imagination. Characters so well written that you just have to keep on reading to find out what, where, when and why!" Amanda M

"A genuine thriller that keeps you guessing to the end with a superb twist. This book moves effortlessly between the past and present throwing you back to university days as though it was yesterday. The characters are so strong and well written they almost walk off the page. It is a real page turner for a debut novel and so I'm looking forward to the next book." Chrissie

"Fantastic read; gripping story and lots of twists waiting for you towards the end. Really recommend Kate's novel, especially for those who love the atmosphere of the snowy mountains and a good psychological thriller." Alexandra Godard

BOOKS BY THIS AUTHOR

Fall Line

"Oh yes, I remember the murder game" he said. "I still play it sometimes."

When Ellie is invited by best friend Kat to join a ski party in a remote Swiss resort, her first instinct is to say no. She doesn't like Kat's new bunch of friends, especially dark, brooding boyfriend Neil.

Reluctantly she agrees and is gradually drawn into the strange, tense circle. Each night, huddled round the fire in the isolated chalet, they play the murder game, taking turns to imagine the most gruesome, twisted way to kill someone in a ski resort.

Many years later, an unexpected invitation arrives. A reunion is planned in the same remote spot. Once again Kat and Ellie find themselves thrown together with the enigmatic group. They are all mature adults now, surely – aren't they?

But Kat has been keeping secrets from Ellie. What really happened on the penultimate day of the holiday all those years ago?

Tensions mount in the chalet. The weather begins to close in and the snow falls steadily. Then, one by one, the guests start to disappear.

Could one of them be carrying out the murders for real?

Printed in Great Britain
by Amazon

61720858R00139